IF THESE WALLS COULD TALK:

A SECRET LOVE AFFAIR

2

WRITTEN BY:

T'ANN MARIE & A. WARD

Published by Tiece Mickens Presents

Constant Contact

Chapter 1

India

I sat there baffled as fuck, as Memphis laughed in my face hard as hell like this was some type of joke.

"Come on baby girl, what type of lame ass nigga you take me for? You think I'm dumb enough to believe that that's my seed you carrying? Where the fuck is Ashton Kutcher? Tell him bring his ass on out, cuz I know damn well I'm being Punk'd!" he said, still laughing hysterically. I took a deep frustrated sigh and folded my arms across my chest.

"Are you done?" I asked with a menacing stare. He was beginning to piss me the fuck off and I wanted to smack fire from his clown ass. Memphis continued to chuckle as he tried to make a straight face.

"Okay, okay, I'm done. But, what makes you so sure that it's my baby, India?" he asked, still smirking.

"Because you were the only person I was sleeping with at the time. I wasn't sleeping with Kingston at all. Every time he would try to have sex, I would make an excuse because I had already been with you. Memphis, I wouldn't be here if I wasn't a hundred percent sure that you are the father. You think I want to be pregnant with another man's baby when I have a whole family at home?" I spat. Memphis took a deep breath, leaned back in his studio chair, and began fondling his chin hairs. There was an awkward silence for a moment; then, he began to speak.

"Okay, well, I guess I'ma be a daddy," he said nonchalantly. "I been wanting a lil shorty for a while now anyway, so shit." He shrugged and threw his hands up carelessly.

"Oh bullshit! Memphis, I'm not keeping this baby; you must be crazy!" I hissed. He had to be the dumbest fool on earth if he thought that that was going to go down. There was way too much at stake. I was friends with his wife and he was friends with my husband; he was asking for death.

"Bullshit, my ass, you keeping my fuckin baby! All this time we been fuckin around, you been hollin you wanna be with a nigga; now is the time. You carrying my baby, girl; it's time we make this shit official. I can't have you out here pregnant and we not together! I ain't that nigga, I'ma be there for mines. So, you might as well kiss that sucker ass nigga Kingston goodbye. You don't need his ass anyway; I just signed a major deal and me, you, and our shorty gon be straight!" he said excitedly. I sat there silent, as I thought about the fucked up situation that I had gotten myself into. I couldn't believe I was dumb enough to be so careless, but that's what good dick would do to you. Memphis picked up the paperwork that I had gotten from the doctor and began reading over it.

"Twelve and a half weeks huh? Pretty soon, we'll be finding out what we're having," he stated with a big smile. "That's wassup! This shit is real, I'm bout to be somebody's daddy!" he continued. His attitude had done a full three-sixty from when I had first told him. At that moment, I didn't know how to feel. I loved Memphis, but I didn't know if I loved him enough to have his child. He was just a thrill for me. Of course, having sex with him so often made me catch some feelings, but I never lost sight of the marriage I shared with my husband. I never meant to make the mistake of getting pregnant.

"Why you so quiet baby? Come here," Memphis said, snapping me from my thoughts. He grabbed me by my left wrist, pulling me onto his lap. "Smile baby, this is a good thing. I told you we straight; I got you through whatever.

Plus, you can't be stressing, you gon stress my son out," he said with a chuckle while rubbing my tummy and kissing the nape of my neck.

"That all sounds good and everything but, Memphis, let's be realistic. What about your wife? What about my husband? Better yet, what about my son!" I said, thinking about KJ. He loved his dad so much and he'd hate me for the rest of his life for destroying our family. Even though he was only three and wouldn't understand, he'd still miss not having his dad around.

"Man, fuck yo husband, he just gotta take this L. My wife," he smacked his lips, "I ain't even worried about her. You giving me something she can't. As long as I let her keep that stupid ass boutique, she'll be iight. I ain't tripping on that muthafucka anyway. That's muthafucka chump change compared to the bread I'm about to start making. And, as far as KJ, he'll be fine, cuz I'ma be the best step daddy ever," he said, planting a soft kiss onto my lips. A quiver began to run down my back, to my vagina. It was just something about this man that drove me insane. He was gutter as hell but sweet, and I loved that shit. He disrespected the broads that came in and out of the studio and talked to people any kind of way but, when it came to me, he was as sweet as sugar. Memphis rubbed the side of my face and I gave him a faint smile.

"I got us baby, I promise," he whispered, staring me in the eyes. He then planted another kiss onto my lips. The kiss got deeper, as I slipped my tongue inside of his mouth and locked his tongue with mine. He began to caress my inner thigh and I could feel my kitty begin to thump. Memphis slipped his hand up my shirt and proceeded to grope my breasts. Caressing my nipples, he made me let out a soft moan. He knew my nipples were my spot and any attention they received sent me into overdrive. I began to grind on his rising wood as I felt it bulging through his jeans. Memphis then picked me up and carried me to the black leather sofa that sat in the corner of the studio room. Lying me on my back, he began to remove my PINK sweatpants. I kicked off my tennis so that he could get them over my feet. Snatching me by my waist, he swiftly pulled me to the edge of the couch and buried his face into my sweet essence. I took a deep gasp, as he sucked my clitoris between his warm lips. He began flickering it in a circular motion, as I grinded against his face. Memphis began slurping this pussy as if it were his last meal.

"Mmmmm," he moaned. That let me know that it tasted good to him. The more he feasted, the closer I felt myself getting closer to climaxing.

"Ooh yes, Memphis baby, suck this pussy!" I moaned, whining my hips faster. He began to shake his face like a Pitbull in my pussy and I damn near lost it. My body began to go into convulsions and I came all over his face. Memphis came up for air, and I sat up and began sucking my juices from his full supple lips. I then began to unbuckle his pants with one hand while fingering my kitty with the other. Memphis stood to his feet and his soldier was standing at attention, right in my face. My mouth instantly began to water at the sight of his big, beautiful, chocolate smooth anaconda. Grabbing it, I began to jack it slowly. I then wrapped my warm lips around it and he immediately began to ooze pre-cum. Sucking up every drop, I began to get my super head on. Swallowing him whole, Memphis' knees began to buckle as his tip touched my tonsils. He grabbed the back of my head and proceeded to fuck my mouth, and I caressed his balls.

"Aarrrgh, fuck!" he groaned as I sucked his dick like my life depended on it. He let me suck a few more minutes, then demanded me to bend over the couch.

"Toot that ass up some more!" he demanded and smacked my ass forcefully. I did as I was told and tooted my ass up more, putting the deepest arch that I could in my back. Memphis bent down and bit both of my ass cheeks before slowly sliding his ten-inch rod into my warm paradise. He continued to stroke until he found his rhythm and began to beat this pussy up. I screamed out in pleasurable pain as he punished me from the back.

"Yes, Memphis, yes, you about to make this pussy cum!" I cried as I clawed at the leather covering the sofa. Memphis put his right leg up onto the couch and climbed deeper into the pussy. My moans grew louder as I began to buss uncontrollably.

"That's right, come all over this dick! You know what to do!" he coached as he gripped my plump ass. "Who pussy is this?" he asked. He then spread my ass cheeks apart and proceeded to long stroke the kitty. I felt like I had died and gone to heaven.

"Yours, it's yours baby! Oh, my gawd, fuck this pussy!" I screamed. Memphis grabbed my hair and began pounding harder and faster. I could feel his dick getting harder and I knew his gun was about to blow.

"Arrgggh! FUCK!" he screamed as he let go inside of me. He pumped a minute longer and pulled out. I fell face first on the couch in exhaustion. Memphis and his bomb ass thug loving was the reason I was in the predicament I was in now.

Chapter 2

Memphis

"Aight baby. I'll get with you later."

I opened the door and let India out the studio. I motioned for the niggas I had recording to come back in. I watched them look at India like a piece of meat, but fuck it; she wasn't mine. She was just another hoe on the list who just happened to be pregnant. Just as I had that thought, it hit me like a sack of potatoes. This motherfucker was possibly pregnant with my offspring. That thought process was quickly killed, as the sound of the group I had recording walked past me.

"Damn, my nigga, you could have let the team have a turn. You got the whole room smelling like sex. We like pussy too, my nigga," one of them mentioned.

I looked at him with a slight grin. "Oh, yeah, my nigga. If you can hit my bitch, you can have her."

Although I had my internal feelings towards the situation with India, the bitch was bad and any nigga that could say that they'd had her ass was winning.

The artist reached out as the two of us bumped fist. "Shit, my nigga, as long as she yours, she like family."

We got back to business. I had my engineer turn their track back on and allowed it to loop around as they pieced together their lyrics. I noticed that my engineer's phone was lighting up on the control board. It was Tahleea calling it. I ignored her call and replied with a text.

Busy right now. Text me or call back later. -Zo

Me fucking with India was perfect. It actually was a blessing. She was a wildcard in the hand of cards that life dealt me. I planned to keep her in my back pocket until I found the most opportune time to play her or in the event her pussy ass husband tried to play me on our deal. That bitch was bait and would be used as such.

My biggest dilemma came with the closeness of her and my wife. In a lot of ways, I was satisfied with the way India was playing everything cool, but the thought of her having too much girl talk with Tahleea blew my mind. I knew that it would only be a matter of time before she came home talking about how India was pregnant and she was having baby fever. I didn't have the time or the patience to deal with her and that shit. With as many babies as the bitch had lost, you would think that she would be tired of trying.

Tahleea was becoming more of a hassle than an asset for me. She didn't understand her place anymore, but her time with me was coming to an end either way. I hoped that the ass whoopings she took would be a sign for her to get out, but the dumb bitch kept ignoring the memo. As my wandering mind raged on, I had to get back on track.

I regained my focus and returned to working on the music at hand. I made some tweaks to the instrumental as the wheels in my head began to start spinning a thousand miles a minute. All I wanted to do was to get through the session so that I could have a moment of silence to process it all.

An hour passed and, finally, we had a song worthy of putting my stamp on. "That's a wrap fellas. Come in here and listen to it."

My engineer placed his finishing touches on the track. Everyone in the room bobbed to the beat as it came blaring out of the speakers.

"My nigga, we got a hit. Preciate that love Memphis," the gentlemen echoed as they heard what was sure to be a radio-ready hit.

One of the homies sparked a blunt and continued moving to the beat as he passed it to me. I hit it twice and felt a sense of accomplishment, not because of the track, but because of everything that was soon to come for me.

The homies left the room with their single in hand, and I sat there alone for a moment with my thoughts. That moment was over in the blink of an eye as there was a knock at the studio door.

"Who is it?" I yelled.

"It's me, nigga, open up," the person replied.

"Who the fuck is me. Come in."

To my surprise, it was an old friend, Hitman. He walked over, bumped my fist, and had a seat.

"What's good my nigga? What brings you to this side of town?" I asked curiously.

"Different day, same shit my nigga. You know me, jugging and finessing."

"I feel that my nigga. For real though, what the fuck you doing out this way?"

He took a deep breath and stroked his beard. He then took his hands and clasped them together before opening his mouth.

"What the fuck is up man?" I questioned again as my patience began to wear thin.

"Memphis, you know I don't like coming to you unless I'm in dire need and, right now, I'm in a bind. I got into bed with some niggas and I got set up for they work. Long story short, I need to borrow about 50 large."

“Got damn man. How many times have I told you not to fuck around? Fifty thousand my nigga? Fuck homie. How much time you got before they on yo head?”

“Man, they already on my head. These niggas say that they gone come after me and everybody I’m acquainted with if they don’t get their money or merchandise. I only came to you because I know that you can help me and you know that you’ll get it back with interest.”

I sat back in my chair and began to spin around. I looked up at the ceiling and shook my head in disbelief. Any other time he would be right but, of all the times for him to catch me down bad, this would have to be it.

“My nigga, you know I can usually always come up on something but, at the present moment, I ain’t got shit. Just let the niggas know that you’ll have the money in the next week or so. If I do this solid for you, I’m going to need a favor.”

He looked up at me, intrigued by my requisition. “Man, if you can make this happen for me, I will do anything you need.”

“Good. I’ll save that favor until it’s needed. In the meantime, stay out of sight and out of mind. Come back and see me in a week. We will be set then.”

He stood to his feet and bumped my fist again before he turned to head for the door. As he exited, I began to ponder on my next moves. I couldn’t continue moving in the manner that I was; I had to become a little bit smarter about shit. I didn’t need to take another loss.

My thoughts on how to get the money began to formulate. I could go into Tahleea’s bank account for the shop and just take it, but that would leave too many questions to answer. The last thing I need to hear was her fucking ass bitching about something else. So, that was out of the question. I thought about going to my business partner Kingston, but the situation was already messy enough with me fucking his wife. So, that was a hell no. I pondered a few moments longer, then had an epiphany.

I didn't think that I would have to play my wildcard so soon, but it was my only option. India was my way to the money. I had to find a way to make her fall deeper for me over the next week and tap into whatever money she had. Shit, with all the money the two of them made, it wasn't going to hurt them at all. I just had to do my part for another week or so and make sure that I didn't do anything to fuck up in the meantime.

I had to get into her mind and kill all the thoughts she had of abortion. That baby was a gold mine and I was gone get my share at all cost. Any false move from me and all this shit would be for nothing though. I couldn't have that happen; I needed to suppress the Memphis I was internally feeling and show her something that she hadn't seen. Although she was cheating on that pussy nigga Kingston, she was still very much attached to him or the thought of him at least. I guess it was just a part of the DNA makeup for females to remain attached. She was accustomed to certain shit. I may not have been able to show her my softer side the way he may, but she wasn't fucking with me for that reason. There was no way in hell that I could allow myself to fuck this shit up.

****

I made it home and noticed that Tahleea's ass was in the bedroom talking to her assistant, Dana. I walked into the room, acknowledged the fact that she was there, and headed into the bathroom.

"Hey girl, he's here. Let me let you go. I will see you tomorrow."

I walked back into the room for a moment prior to her hanging up and looked at her.

"Who the fuck is he? Bitch, I got a name."

"I'm sorry baby. I wasn't thinking before I said it. I know you got a name," she replied.

"Yeah, aight. Don't do that shit again or I'ma give you a reason to say my shit." She nodded in agreement, then attempted to change the subject.

"How was your day?" she asked.

"Long."

"What did you do?"

"Worked."

"Ok is something wrong? Am I bothering you or something."

"You good." She stopped asking questions and went back to her phone. I headed into the bathroom and began to wash India's pussy off my body. Before I could get into the shower, I called for my wife.

"Aye. Tahleea, come here." She popped her head in the door and peeped in.

"Yeah, what's up?"

"Come here," I replied.

She walked over towards the shower and I reached out to grab her arm.

"I'm good baby," she said hesitantly.

"I didn't ask you if you was good. Get yo ass in here." She looked at me sideways for a moment, until I opened the shower curtain and clenched my jaw.

"Don't make me ask twice. My dick need some attention."

"Memphis, really?" She turned her head to the side.

"Get the fuck in," I impetrated. Taking off her clothes, she did as I asked, and I pushed her chest flat against the walls of the shower. I slapped my dick against her plump ass a couple times to get it aroused before I turned her back around.

"Hit yo knees and suck my dick," I demanded.

I could see the tears forming in her eyes, but I didn't give a shit. I'd become quite used to the emotional creature she'd become. I had no remorse as she bobbed and weaved her head, sucking India's juices off my dick. It took about 10 minutes before I pulled my dick out of her mouth and sprayed her face with my kids. Hell, that was the only place they seemed safe with her. She cleaned herself off and stepped out of the shower.

"Aye, after I finish this shower and nap, I'm going to need yo phone for a minute. I got a few moves to make and can't be out here without one. So, until I get another throw-away, I'll jus borrow yours. So, text ya lil boyfriends and tell em you can't talk to em for a couple hours because daddy home."

Chapter 3

Tahleea

I sat on the edge of the bed as I watched Memphis sleeping. My mind raced, as I thought of the many different ways I could off his sick ass. I thought about putting a pillow over his face and sitting on it, so he could smother to death. Then, I thought that would be too difficult. He could have easily woken up and threw me off him. His ass was strong as fuck, and I was nowhere near a match for him. I looked at the lamp sitting on our nightstand, and I immediately had flashes of me bashing his head in with the muthafucka until I killed him, but I knew that would be too bloody. Lastly, I had visions of me pouring gasoline all over the muthafuckin house and him, striking a match, and standing out front smoking a blunt as I watched the muthafucka burn to smithereens. No, I didn't smoke weed, but it would be the perfect reliever after some shit like that. As I sat there still pondering on how to cancel this bitch ass nigga, my cell began to ring. Gazing at the screen, I noticed that it was my baby boo, Dana. Walking out of the bedroom, I headed downstairs so that I could talk privately. Plus, I didn't want to risk waking that nutty muthafucka up and have him trying to fight me for talking too loud.

"Hello," I whispered into the phone as I creeped down the steps to the living room.

"Hey boss lady, what the hell you whispering for?" she asked curiously.

"Uggh, how many times have I told you to quit it with this boss lady shit? Call me by my name, damn," I cursed her. She pissed me off with that shit. We were friends and she contributed just as much to my business as I did. There was no need for her to keep addressing me as boss lady. "And I was whispering because Memphis is sleep and

I wasn't trying to wake him. I'm downstairs in the living room now, so we good," I told her. Dana scoffed.

"As long as you're the boss of Cuteazz Couture, your name is boss lady. What does us being friends have to do with anything? Nothing!" she spat. "And fuck Memphis and his sleep! I'll come over there with a blow horn and blow that muthafucka in his ear, and his bitch ain't gone do shit!" she snapped. Just the mention of that nigga's name boiled her blood.

"Girl, you ass is crazy ass hell! What's up though, what you doing?" I asked her.

"Nothing, bored as fuck! I was calling to see if you wanted to step out with me for a little minute?" she asked.

"Uhm, I don't know Dana; I don't feel like hearing this nigga's mouth," I said hesitantly.

"Girl, fuck him! You are a grown ass woman. He can't decide what you can and can't do. Plus, it's not even late. It's only fifteen minutes after eight. I'll be there by nine, I promise," she hissed. I held the phone for a few seconds and thought about it. She was right. I was grown as hell, and I could do and go anywhere I damn sure pleased.

"Okay bitch, I'll be ready by nine," I assured her.

"Yessss, boss lady! We about to have a fun night; let me go, so I can hurry up and finish getting ready. I'll be there soon," she chirped.

"Wait, where we going? How do I need to dress?" I asked. I wanted to make sure I was dressed for the occasion.

"Get sexy! We turning heads tonight biiiih!" she said excitedly.

"Oh lawd, you really trying to get me killed huh?" I asked her. She knew damn well Memphis wasn't letting me out of his sight in shit sexy.

"Girl, that pussy boy ain't gonna do shit! I wish he would, I got a new baby today and I can't wait to let her rip. That muthafucka betta stay in his lane, or his ass gon be spending his nights in the nearest trauma center!" Dana spat, referring to her new gun.

"Jeezus, okay bitch. Your loony ass stay ready to shoot some damn body. I'll be ready when you get here, with ya ratchet ass!" I giggled.

"You love my ratchet ass though! I'm the best friend you'll ever have and I'm not gone let nobody fuck with my friend. Period! But, bye, I'll see you in a minute!" She blew a kiss threw the phone and hung up. I giggled as I made my way back up the stairs so that I could get ready. Dana was exactly right. She was the best friend that I'd ever had and I loved her to pieces. There was nothing I wouldn't do for her and vice versa. She was the true definition of a rider, and I wouldn't trade her for the world.

Walking into my closet, I skimmed through my clothes for something to wear. I had already taken a shower about an hour prior, so all I had to do was get dressed. Pulling out a black, lace bodycon dress that I had bought from Bebe a few months ago and never got to wear, and a pair of black red bottoms, I had my outfit for the night. I quietly grabbed my makeup bin and everything that I would need to prepare myself and went into another bedroom in the house. After beating my face for the gawds, I commenced to slipping my dress on. I stood in my full-length mirror and admired the way that it hugged my curves. I could tell that my dieting and workouts were working because my little pudge was almost nonexistent, and my booty was rounder and fatter. I played around in the mirror as I made my booty cheeks jump one at a time. I giggled hard as hell; I was really feeling myself. I was certain that I would break necks tonight, not just turn them.

Grabbing my skin so soft body oil, I proceeded to oil my thick ass, blemish free legs. After, I pulled off my bonnet and let my 22, 24, & 26-inch Malaysian bundles flow. It was already curled, so I just ran my fingers through it until it was just how I liked it. I then threw on some jewelry to complement my outfit and sprayed some Dolce and Gabbana all over my body. I waited to put my heels on until I got into the car. I wanted to get out of the house before Memphis woke up and started tripping. If he seen me dressed the way I was, my ass wouldn't have made to the door, let alone out. Checking my phone, it was 8:53 pm. Hitting the envelope icon, I shot Dana a text to see how close she was.

Ready! How close are you? -Tahleea

It took her no time to reply.

At the light about to turn on your street, come outside. -Dana

"Shit!" I said to myself as I gathered my things and threw them into my Prada bag. Dana's ass wasn't playing, she was before time. Scrolling to Kingston's name in my phone, I clicked on it and sent him a text as well.

Stepping out with Dana for the night. Memphis will have my phone since he doesn't have one right now, so don't text back or call. I'll call you from Dana's phone later. I love you! -Tahleea

I then quickly erased the message, his name, and saved his number under Dana's name, just in case that nigga tried to be nosey and snoop through my phone. Grabbing my purse and heels, I tiptoed to our bedroom, sat my phone on the nightstand, and crept out of the house. Memphis having my phone was actually a good thing because he wouldn't be able to call and see where I was. After quietly closing the front door, I locked it behind me and made my way to Dana's car. When I hopped in, Dana was in the mirror of the visor applying some red matte lipstick onto her lips.

"Hey boss lady!" she greeted me.

"Hey pooh, you look cute," I complimented her, taking the socks I had on off and putting my Louboutins on. Dana was rocking a nude colored mini dress with a cute brown vest and some brown, thigh-high, open-toed boots that laced up the middle. Her hair was slicked up into a neat bun and her baby hair laid perfectly around her edges. Dana was a cute chocolate doll. She really put you in the mind of Keisha from off of Belly.

"Thank you, boo, I try!" she said, placing the cap back onto her lipstick and flipping her visor back closed. She then looked over at me.

"Well, I be damn! How the fuck did you manage to get out of the house looking like that?! Damn, boss lady! You lucky I don't mix business and pleasure, jeezus Christ!" she said, roaming her eyes over me from head to toe. I immediately scoffed and chuckled.

"Oh, gawd Dana, what is that suppose to mean?" I asked her crazy ass.

"It means you look good as fuck! You making a bitch think strange thangs!" She giggled. "I've never seen you dressed like this before. Do you have on panties!?" she asked, acting as if she was trying to get a peek.

"Oh, my God, Dana, did you really just ask me that?" I chuckled.

"What? I jus asked a question!" She laughed.

"Dana, just drive!" I told her. "And, if you must know, no, I do not have on any panties!" I shot.

"Oooh, I knew it! Let me see!" she stated. My mouthed dropped in shock. I couldn't believe Dana was coming on to me. I didn't even know she swung that way.

"Dana, bitch, just drive! You being real gay right now!" I laughed.

"Okay, damn! Bitches get in the car looking and smelling all edible and expect a bitch not to turn homo! You shol right!" She laughed, putting the car in drive and pulling off.

Chapter 4

Kingston

The thought of responding to the text Tahleea sent crossed my mind, but it may have been in the best interest of the both of us if I didn't at the moment. There were so many things going on at one time that my brain couldn't process them all at once. Her giving Memphis her phone for the night actually worked out in my favor. It was one less thing to stress about. It gave me time to focus on a plan of attack to ensure that her and I would be as one sooner, rather than later.

I sat on the couch with KJ in my lap watching tv, when I heard India walk through the doors of our home.

"Mommy!" KJ yelled with jubilation as he jumped off my lap and darted towards her in a full sprint.

I paused the program he and I were watching to go over and greet India. I noticed the clock on the wall and it showed that it was a little bit past 9 pm. I walked over and gave her a hug and kiss on the cheek.

"Long day at work?" I asked her.

"Something like that baby. I don't feel too well. I'm kind of tired. I think that I am going to turn in early."

"But, you just got here…"

"I know baby. I am sorry. I will make it up to you. I promise. I've just had a really long and hard day. All I want to do is lay down."

I decided against arguing with her. Instead, I reached down and picked KJ up. His face showed disappointment, but he understood at such a young age that his parents' careers sometimes drained them of life.

"Hey big man, give mama a kiss so that she can get some sleep. We will get some ice cream and finish the show."

He reached out for her and embraced her with a warm hug. Before the both of us knew it, she had vanished into our master bedroom. KJ and I headed back towards the living area where we were.

"Daddy."

"What's up KJ?"

"Mommy smells funny."

"KJ, that's not nice man. She's had a long day. Sometimes, adults work so hard that they work up a slight odor."

"But, daddy, she smells really weird. She doesn't smell like her usual perfume. She stinks."

I sat KJ still and got him situated with a bowl of ice cream for a moment. I started the show we were watching again and allowed the tv to temporarily babysit him, while I went into the bedroom and checked on India.

Her clothes were draped over the bedroom floor as I heard the shower running. KJ was right. I didn't notice her scent prior to him saying something, but her clothes had the distinct smell of burned tar and marijuana. I walked over to the bathroom entrance and gazed at her through the glass shower.

"Everything ok?" I asked.

I must have spooked her because I heard her body wash hit the floor. "Yeah, everything is fine Kingston. What do you need?"

"I don't need anything India. Can I not admire my wife from a far? I don't have to have an appointment to do that, do I? How was your day?"

I could see her attempting to look through the steamy glass door at me.

"It was fine Kingston. Like I told you, it was just extremely long. I am worn out."

"I know baby. I got that much. Are you ok? Is there anything you want to tell me or talk to me about?"

She stopped the shower and the room grew silent, as I awaited an answer. "What do you mean Kingston. I am fine. We are fine. I don't think I have anything that I haven't told you."

I ran my hand over my beard and took a deep breath. "Come on India. I know you better than that. If you've started smoking again, that's all you have to say. There is no need to lie about it. I ain't here to judge you, but I am here to help you through whatever stress that you feel. I don't want you back to a pack a day. So, what's really good?"

She opened the glass door to the shower and wrapped her body and hair up in a towel. She looked into my direction, still slightly confused, as to say my statement was invalid. In return, I walked out of the bathroom, over to the pile of clothes she left in the middle of our bedroom floor, and grabbed her blazer. I took another sniff of the jacket, just to make sure that I wasn't tripping.

"KJ smelled it on you first. So, again, I ask is there something that you want to tell me?"

She gave me a deceptive smirk and looked at me with her head slightly tilted. "Can't get anything past you two, huh?"

I shook my head no. Her smile grew larger as she took the towel from her head and began to blotch her hair with it.

"Kingston, I am not smoking. This is probably from the client that I was with earlier. He was stressed out and he smokes like a train. We were in close proximity so, of course, I am going to have some of the remnants of what he was smoking in my clothes. Thus, the shower. I was well aware that I carried a scent with me." She shook her head in disbelief and turned to face the mirror.

"In that case, I apologize for even bringing it up. I just want to make sure that we're on the same page and that we don't have any hidden secrets."

She looked at me in the reflection of the mirror and shook her head. I turned away and left her alone to finish what she needed to finish. I walked back into the living room, where I found KJ already asleep with a half-eaten bowl of ice cream. I picked him up and took him into his room. I laid him down, kissed his forehead, and said a small prayer over him.

"Father in heaven, I ask as humbly as I know how that you keep my son from hurt harm and danger. If you see it in your will for him to have trials and tribulations in his life, I ask that they be minimal in pain but great in lessons. I also ask that you keep him in good health and good spirit. Protect his heart, watch over his soul, and I will do my part to raise him in your likeness during his earthly walk. It's in your son's name, I pray. AMEN."

I stood over him for a few moments to make sure that he was in a deep sleep before walking out of his room. Closing his door, I took a deep breath and laid my head upon it. Too many thoughts consumed me. My son was pure and innocent. He was the part of me that was pure and cleansed.

I shook my thoughts and headed down the hallway. I looked at the mess in the living room and decided that it was best to clean things up. As I took the half-eaten bowl of ice cream from KJ into the kitchen, India walked in, in nothing more than my t-shirt and startled me. I simply looked into her direction and smiled.

"That's a good look on you, kid."

She smiled back and proceeded to reach into the refrigerator. She pulled out a bottle of Fiji water and took a massive gulp before she returned her attention to me.

"This used to be my favorite look; now it's just a comfortable one for me." She shrugged her shoulders and made her way out of the kitchen. I stood still momentarily, trying to understand her statement, but nothing came to mind that rationalized it. I finished washing the dish and headed into our bedroom. India was on her side, looking at something on her phone with a smile on her face. As she looked up and saw my face, her demeanor began to change.

"Man, what the hell is wrong with you?"

"Nothing is wrong Kingston. I'm just tired. I told you I wasn't feeling well. Just leave it there."

If looks could kill, she was six feet under dancing with the devil. I didn't make another mention to it. I simply grabbed my headphones, plugged them into my phone, and listened to my music. Something was going on with India, but I was so far disconnected from my marriage that it didn't faze me as it once would have.

I began to go through my contact list, preparing to text Tahleea, and then it hit me that I couldn't.

"Fuck!" I mumbled to myself as I put my phone down and adjusted my pillow. The one motherfucker to take my mind off all this shit was busy doing who knows what. She was a free agent for the night and I was stuck in the house with the wicked witch of the Westside. I tried my best to make the best of the situation as I zoned out, looking into the darkness of the room.

Chapter 5

Tahleea

Dana and I pulled up in front of Q Nightclub on Broadway around fifteen after ten, and the line was wrapped around the building on both sides.

“Damn, it’s packed as fuck tonight! We really about to stand in this long ass line?” I looked at her with the screw face. She had to be out of her damn mind if she thought I was about to stand in that line in these eight-inch Louboutins; wasn’t going to happen. Dana busted out into laughter.

“Tuh, boss lady, you must don’t know who the fuck I am! Well, you gon learn today! Come on, let’s go!” she told me. Hopping out of her cranberry Beamer, she threw her keys to valet and we headed straight for the door.

“What’s up Dana, baby? I been waiting on that ass!” This big, buff, handsome, chocolate, bald bouncer said as we approached. He looked as if he lived in the gym, and he was tatted up like a biker boy. The tight shirt he sported showed off every bulge in his arms and every ripple of his six pack in his stomach. The man was fine as hell.

“Hey Trech, what’s up love?” she said, hugging him while planting a light kiss onto his cheek. He returned the kiss as he held her around the waist.

“Damn Dana, you so soft and you smell so good! When you gonna stop playing with a nigga and fuck with me?” he asked while looking her in the face, still holding on to her by the hips. Dana slightly chucked.

“Never! I keep telling yo ass Trech, I’m not no side bitch. You happily married with three whole children; plus, I know your wife. I don’t get down like that!” she spat. The bouncer smacked his lips and rolled his eyes to the top of his head.

"Aw, here you go! Enjoy your night sexy ladies," he said, opening the rope to let us in.

"Yea, I figured you didn't want to hear that!" Dana giggled, leading the way into the club.

Any other time before now, the statement Dana made to Trech about not wanting to be a side bitch would've made me feel some type of way, but I knew deep down the events that were about to transpire. I was no longer the side bitch, and Kingston would soon be all mine. Just thinking about that man gave me butterflies. I wanted to call him so bad, just to hear his voice. I would've rather been laid up with him than to be in the club any day, and I knew he would've wanted the same. When we approached the bar, Dana proceeded to order drinks for us.

"Hey, can I get six shots of mango Cîroc?" she yelled over the music to the bartender. The bartender nodded her head and commenced to making the drinks.

"Six? Bitch, it's only two of us!" I told her, looking at her confused as hell.

"Uhhm, I know," she replied nonchalantly.

"So, who you ordering all of those shots for?"

"Us! You do everything in threes when you with me! We about to have fun, drink up!" Dana handed me the shots, then turned to pay and tip the bartender. We threw the shots back together, then headed for the dance floor. I had never had mango Cîroc before, but I had to admit I liked it, a lot. When we made it to the dance floor, Dana and I began to slang our hair and sway our hips to Jeezy & Chris Brown's new hit song, *Pretty Diamonds.* It was my shit and the song itself made me feel sexy as fuck. I could feel the three shots of Cîroc kicking in, as I turned around and began to grind my fatty on Dana. Grabbing me by my waist, she began to dance with me. Slightly bending over, I looked back at her as I jiggled my booty cheeks against her abdomen. Dana began to caress it as we grinded on each other until the song went off. Making our way back to the bar, Dana ordered six more shots of Cîroc. As we waited for the bartender to make them, we were approached by the two sexiest studs I'd ever seen in my life. I wasn't into chicks with dicks, but I couldn't front; these two she-he's made a bitch think some strange thangs.

"How you sexy ladies doin tonight? I couldn't help but to be mesmerized by the beautiful performance you two were giving on the dance floor; the shit was sexy as fuck! Do you ladies mind if I pay for your drinks?" one of them stated. The Young MA looking muthafucka was serving nothing but sex appeal. I had to pep talk myself because I couldn't believe I was having nasty thoughts about a girl/boy. It had to be the damn Cîroc talking.

"Nah, we straight. We can pay for our own drinks!" Dana spat, looking the two studs up and down.

"Ooh shit!" the light skin one that looked like Young MA's clone said, as she licked her lips and rubbed her hands together. "You chocolate, fine, and feisty, just like I like em. What's your name ma?" she asked. Dana scoffed as she rolled her eyes.

"Clearly, I'm not interested. I'm just here to have drinks and a good time with my friend, nothing more," she snapped. The bartender sat our drinks onto the bar and Dana tried paying him, but the stud handed over her black card first. After he swiped it, he handed her a receipt and a pen. The stud then wrote him a hundred-dollar tip and signed her name.

“If these ladies order anything else Ronnie, put it on my tab,” she told the bartender. She then turned her attention back to Dana. “Well, finish enjoying the night with your friend sexy. I just wanted to buy your fine ass drinks, Ms. Dana. Yea, I already know your name. You ladies have a good night. By the way, I’m Sunny. Different day, another circumstance, I’ll see you again beautiful!” She winked her eye at Dana, then walked off. Dana looked at me and I, at her.

“Biiiih, who was that? Let me find out!” I said, grinning hard as hell. It was clear that ole babe was feeling the fuck out of my girl, and she was acting shady as hell.

“Girl, the hell if I know, but I ain’t feeling her! She can keep it pushing though. I don’t even know how she know my fucking name!” Dana spat, rolling her eyes as she handed me my three shots. We threw one back together.

“Cleary, she’s seen you around and has been checking for you. You gone see her again, watch and see what I tell you,” I told her, proceeding to throw back my second shot. Dana scoffed and rolled her eyes.

“Whateva!” she hissed, then threw her shot back as well. I chuckled at her ass; she was really being stuck up. We threw our last shot back and headed back to the dance floor. We went back and forth from the bar to the dance floor all night long, partying all the way up until the club closed. Giggling and stumbling out to the club, we made small talk as we waited for valet to roll up with Dana’s car.

“I’m so hungry; I need something to put on this liquor before I be sick!” I told her.

“Me too, boss lady. Ain’t too much open, it’s 3 a.m. Where we gon go?” she replied with the hiccups.

"I don't know, but I'm starving and I'm not ready to go back home just yet," I shot.

"Uhhm, well, we can go back to my house and I can whip us up some chicken and waffles," she offered.

"Bitch, please! Yo ass too drunk to be trying to cook anything!" I laughed at her ass. The heffa could barely keep her balance and she was talking about cooking. Hell, I was seriously contemplating on if I should get in the car with her ass or call us an Uber.

"Boss lady, please, I'm not drunk! I'm tipsy as fuck but not drunk. I'm fully focused and can do anything I could if I was sober," she stated. I simply shook my head and chuckled at her.

When valet had finally pulled around with her car, she tipped him and we got it. Pulling off into the night, Dana turned on some Ty Dolla Signs and we cruised, jamming all the way to her place. When we arrived, she pulled into her two-car garage, and we got out and headed for the door.

"Welcome to my place, boss lady. It might not be as big and pretty as your house, but it's nice and cozy," she said while opening the door, and we stepped in.

"Girl, hush! This is nice," I said when we got inside of her spacious, squeaky clean kitchen. She had it decorated really nice in red, black, and white chef designs, and all her appliances were stainless steel. It was really cute and I wanted to see more of the house.

"This is nice Dana, give me a tour," I told her. She did as I asked and showed me around. Her three-bedroom, two-and-a-half-bathroom house was beautiful, and she had it decorated perfectly. It was definitely more than enough room for it just to be her living there. She even had a huge basement with a bar in it and a big ass, fenced-off back yard.

"Boss lady, you can sit at the kitchen island while I go get out of these clothes. Make yourself at home and help yourself to anything you like," she told me. "You want a big t-shirt or something, so you can get out of that dress and get comfortable?" she asked.

"Yes, please! That would be great," I accepted.

"Okay, I'll be right back," she stated, disappearing off into her bedroom. I sat at the kitchen island in silence, as I waited for her to come back. My mind began to wonder, as I thought about the consequences I would face when I made it back home. I knew Memphis would be thirty-eight hot about me sneaking out and staying gone all night. A part of me really didn't give a fuck about his feelings, but the other part of me gave a fuck about what I would be feeling when I walked through the door. As I thought deeper, I came up with a plan. First thing in the morning, I was going to head to Sprint and buy him a new phone and take it home with me. That would take his mind off my whereabouts, and I could even get my fucking phone back. Interrupting my thoughts, Dana came back into the kitchen wearing a pair of blue, laced boy shorts that barely covered her smooth chocolate plump ass, and a white mini t-shirt that exposed her erect, pierced nipple prints. She was beautiful as hell, and her dark flawless skin had a natural smooth glow. Walking over to me, she handed me an oversized t-shirt.

"So, you want me to make chicken and waffles, or you want me to whip up a couple of burgers?" she asked while walking over to the fridge, opening it.

"It don't matter; whatever you feel like doing. I'm gonna go in the bathroom and get out of these clothes," I told her, standing up from the island stool and heading for the bathroom. It took me no time to change and I was on my way back into the kitchen. Dana was seasoning the ground beef and packing hamburger parties when I arrived.

"You need some help boo?" I asked her, sitting back at the island.

"Nah, I'm straight. It ain't gone take me no time to fry these thangs," she replied, throwing the burgers onto the George Foreman grill and closing it down. She then proceeded to wash her hands. After she dried them, she went over to the freezer and opened it up.

"Look what I goooooot!!" she said with a big grin, pulling out a fifth of frosted mango Cîroc. I simply shook my head and busted into giggles.

"Oh gawd, bitch, haven't you had enough? We had like ten shots apiece at the club!" I stated.

"Oh, shut up! Do you want some or not?" she asked, cocking her head to the side.

"Now, what kind of friend would I be to let you drink alone?" I replied.

"My nigga!" she said, turning to grab some glasses from the cabinet. After, she poured us up a nice double shot. We sipped and chit chatted as we waited for the burgers to get done. When they were done, we ate and cleaned up our mess. Grabbing the bottle and glasses, we made our way to Dana's bedroom, where we continued to sip and talk.

"Boss lady, can I ask you a personal question?" Dana's drunk ass asked, burning a hole through me.

"Yea, sure. But why you gotta look at me like that?" I asked, chuckling. Knowing her, it wasn't any telling what the hell she was about to ask my ass.

"Have you ever been with a woman?" she blurted, and I immediately busted into laughter. I knew she was about to ask me some outrageous shit. Her name wouldn't be Dana if she didn't. "What's so funny? Just answer the question, damn!" she spat.

"I just knew your ass was about to ask something crazy. But no, Dana, I've never been with a woman," I replied honestly, taking another sip of my Cîroc.

"Have you ever thought about it?" she shot back. I took a deep sigh.

"Uhm, I have before, but then it immediately escapes my brain. Like, I see a lot of sexy women on a daily and be like damn, she bad, but I just can't see myself eating the box!" I chuckled.

"Well, would you let a woman eat your box?" she asked with a raised brow.

"Uhm, maybe. It depends."

"Depends on what?"

"Oh gawd, Dana, where are you going with this? Why are you asking me these things?" I asked curiously, even though I knew where she was hinting at.

"Let me suck your pussy!" she flat out asked.

"What?!" I giggled, flabbergasted that she asked so bluntly.

"Let me suck it. I want to see what you taste like boss lady," she continued.

"What? No, uh un, we can't do that," I told her. As much I wouldn't have mind bussing in her pretty little face, I couldn't let that happen.

"Why, you scared?"

"No, I'm not. It just wouldn't be right. Dana, we have to work together; did you forget that?" I asked, refreshing her drunk ass memory.

"Uhm, so! What that mean?" she said nonchalantly. "I just want to eat your pussy; I didn't ask you to marry me or no shit like that. I don't want you to return the favor or none of that. I just want to see what you look like when you cum," she confessed. Just hearing her say those last few words gave my pussy a pulse. I had always wondered what it would feel like to get head from a woman. After hearing so many stories about how it was the best orgasm you'd ever experience, I was curious as hell.

"I don't know Dana. I like our relationship and I don't want to complicate it or make it awkward," I told her. "You're my girl and I don't want this to mess up our friendship." Dana fell out into laughter.

"It's okay boss lady. I understand; you're scared. It's cool," she said, sipping from her glass. I immediately scoffed.

"I'm far from scared. Like I said, I just don't want to complicate things," I told her again.

"What is there to complicate? We will still remain friends, we will still work together, nothing will change. Only thing is, I will know what that pussy tastes like," she said seductively, reaching over and softly pinching one of my nipples. A chill began to run down my spine as I bit down on my bottom lip and let out a soft moan. I could feel the flood gates between my legs getting ready to open. Dana then leaned in and placed a soft kiss onto my lips.

"So, you gon let me taste it or nah?" she asked, looking me into my eyes. Giving in, I slowly shook my head yes. Dana rose from the bed and placed her cup onto the nightstand. Slowly walking over to me, she kneeled in front of me. My hands and legs began to shake, as a sense of nervousness began to come over me.

"Oh gawd, boss lady, would you relax; you shaking like a stripper!" Dana chuckled. I busted into laughter as I threw my left hand over my face in embarrassment.

"Okay, damn, Dana. I'm nervous, sheesh!" I spat, throwing back the last little gulp of liquor I had left in my glass. I then reached over and sat my glass on the nightstand next to hers.

"Just lay back," she ordered, and I did as I was told. Dana began to plant soft kisses between my thick thighs, sending me into overdrive. The closer her lips got to my kitty, the harder my clit began to throb. Diving right in, she locked her lips around my pulsating pearl and I let out a deep, exasperating gasp. The feeling of her soft, warm, plump lips against my pussy was indescribable. She began to flicker her warm tongue softly and slowly against my pearl tongue and, just that fast, I could feel my orgasm approaching. I didn't know what super powers her mouth possessed, but no one had ever made my kitty feel this good from oral stimulation.

"Oooh, boss lady, you taste so good!" Dana moaned as she continued to munch on my box. I grinded my pelvis against her face, as my clit felt as if it was going to explode.

"Aahh fuck, Dana, baby I'm about to cum!" I squealed as my head began to get lighter and my ears began to pop. Dana planted her face deeper into my pussy and began to shake her head like a Pitbull. I arched my back up off the bed, as I let all of myself go into her mouth. My body began to go into convulsions, as Dana continued to slurp up all my bodily fluids. When she finished, she planted a soft kiss onto my pussy lips. I laid there exhausted and speechless as my legs tingled uncontrollably. Dana had just given me the best head of my life. This was and had to be the first, and last time.

Chapter 6

Kingston

Morning came and I found myself stuck in my natural routine. With my mug of green tea sitting on the desk, I opened my email and began reviewing the activity from the previous day. As I read through the emails, one captured my eye. It was from my attorney. I printed it off and immediately felt the day shifting into the right gears.

Everything is finalized as you wished. Congrats on yet another business venture my friend.

S. Sterling
Attorney at Law

I sat back in my chair and printed off all the attachments. I began to review everything to ensure that there were no loop holes. The transferal of ownership involving Memphis' business was complete. There was a moment of clarity for me, which meant that there would soon be the same for Tahleea. Phase one of my process was almost complete. I sat back in my chair and kicked my feet up on the desk with a smile that could blind a room. The nigga had completely fucked himself. Just as the thoughts of him crumbling at my feet crossed my mind, I received a text from Tonya, my secretary, who was out on Maternity leave.

Mr. Kennedy I hope I'm not interrupting anything but I need to speak with you as soon as you have the time. Its urgent, the sooner the better. -Tonya

I wasted no time replying and followed up with an urgent text of my own.

Whenever you need to talk, I am here. I am still at the office so if you want to call or come by, I am here until 5. -Kingston

Before I could place the phone down on my desk, it vibrated once more. Tonya decided that it would be best to come into the office and see me. I paged out to the desk of my new secretary, Serenity, and informed her to clear my schedule around noon. She did as she was asked and proceeded to get back to work.

About ten minutes passed and I began to read over emails when I heard a knock at my door. I looked down at my Rose Gold Armani watch, then looked at my schedule on the computer. I wasn't expecting anyone at the time.

"Come in!" I yelled, beginning to stand to my feet.

As the door swung open, I began making my way closer to it.

"Hey Mr. Kingston, I am so sorry. There is a woman claiming to be your wife, demanding to speak with you. I wasn't for sure if she was or not, so I told her to wait out in the lobby."

My face turned pale for a moment. It wasn't like India to make an appearance to the office unannounced, let alone in the middle of the day when she should have been at work.

"You did your part. Please send her in."

Serenity took a deep breath and ran her hand over her hair nervously, as if she'd done something wrong. As she walked away, I turned back towards my desk to put all the paperwork on it away. I heard India before the door even cracked.

"All this could have been avoided if you would have just let me up here. Did he tell you I was his wife? Yes? Oh, ok, I thought so, dumb ass girl."

The door swung open and India walked through with her Coach wristlet dangling from her wrist.

"I want that bitch fired. I been here for damn near 30 minutes arguing with this dumb ass girl. All she had to do was come ask or, better yet, page you. I want her gone. She is going to fuck things up here. I wouldn't be surprised if she hasn't already."

I looked at India as she continued with her semi-rant and I sat back in my seat.

"Baby… it's done. Now, relax," I stated in her direction. I looked down at my watch once more, then back up at India. "So, what do I owe the pleasure of my wife popping up on me randomly in the middle of the day, when she should be at work?"

She took a deep breath and switched her crazy switch back off. "I wasn't feeling too well, so I decided to take the rest of the day off. I thought I'd pop up on you and make sure that you were behaving. I know I was a bitch last night and I apologize," she stated with a huge smile on her face.

"Behaving huh? I always behave baby. You ain't got shit to worry about on this end," I replied, lying through my teeth. "Nonetheless, you could have apologized over the phone. So, I am to believe that there is more to this situation that I am being led on to believe."

Before she could utter any words, my phone began buzzing on my desk's top. I walked over to it and opened the text message. I picked it up and began to read over the text message. It was from Tahleea. My facial expression must have changed for the positive because India took exception to it.

"Who is that? They seemed to have put a smile on your face."

I couldn't come up with a lie fast enough.

"Let me see who it is."

I looked down at my phone and smirked. I unlocked the phone and handed it to her. If this was the way to get away from our situation, then so be it. She looked up at me and shook her head.

"You know what, Kingston. I really didn't expect you to give it to me, but the fact that you did let me know that you don't have any dirt or anything to hide. You're such a good boy. I don't need this. Here baby, I trust you."

I took the phone back and continued to read the message that came from Tahleea.

Aye, tell Tahleea to call me or get her ass home ASAP. I got to talk to her about some shit. -Tahleea.

I looked at the message, confused about why the hell I got the text clearly designated for someone else. The fact that this nigga had the audacity to text me, of all people, blew my mind and almost sent a chill over my body. For a second, I thought the nigga was smart enough to figure out that me and his girl were more than just friends. Upon second thought, I figured Tahleea was surely smart enough to not have my name and number in plain sight, given the fact that she gave him the phone. I took the safe route and texted back OK. I deleted my signature so that wouldn't tip him off.

My attention returned to India, as she sat in the chairs across from my desk playing on her phone. She looked up at me for a moment, then stopped.

"Oh, you done. You got time for your wife now?"

"Man, you really been on one lately."

"Motherfu… you know what, you right baby. I have been. I said I was going to stop being a bitch to you and, damn it, that's what I'm going to do."

I looked at her and noticed that her eyes were starting to darken and she was developing bags under them. "India, have you talked to yo mama lately?"

"No… why?"

"The last time you acted like this and started to have a change in appearance, you were pregnant with KJ. So, do I need to go get a pregnancy test?"

She got quiet, then looked down at her phone. I could see her texting someone before her head sprung back up.

"Kingston, you're being delusional. We've fucked a handful of times lately, if that. Do you really think I could be pregnant? When KJ was conceived, we were like two savage animals in heat. There is no way in hell I could be."

I sat back in my chair and really began to think on her answer. She was right; we hadn't been fucking as much as we did before.

"Let's not put that shit on us right now. Anyway, you want to go grab a bite before you get too caught up in anything?"

I looked down at my watch and noticed that the time was moving rather quickly. If I did decide to go eat, I had roughly 45 minutes before I had to be back to meet with a client. "If we can make it quick, then yes, we can."

"Well, bring your ass on. I'm hungry."

I looked at her and laughed, as I went to open the door for her. "Yep. I'm getting that pregnancy test. You ain't about to tell me yo ass ain't pregnant."

She lifted her hand and flipped me off. As we made our way down the hallway towards the elevators, I heard it open and, to my surprise, it was Tonya. She looked up at me and I at her. India's face lit up with excitement.

"Tonya, girl, you look good. You can't even tell you've had a baby."

"Mrs. Kennedy, thank you. I didn't know you were here. How are you?"

"I'm good girl. Is this the little one?"

She shook her head yes. I stood frozen until the doors of the elevator began to close on her. I placed my hand in front of the motion sensor and finally greeted Tonya.

"Tonya, you're early. I wasn't expecting you until noon."

"Well, I was already in the area and I knew my meeting would be brief. I didn't want to waste and entire time slot for what I needed to talk to you about."

India looked at me, then looked at Tonya, then back at me. "Well, don't just stand there, fool. Go talk to the woman. We need her back cause that other lil girl got to go. I meant that shit. Go handle your business. I'll be in the car waiting."

She kissed my cheek, then got on the elevator. I placed all my attention onto Tonya and the baby that was in the detachable car seat. She reached down to pick him up, but I stopped her and grabbed the seat and led her into my office.

She had a seat in the exact seat my wife just moved her ass from. The room was filled with an awkward silence. As I fixed my lips to try to speak, Tonya's words beat me to the punch.

"Mr. Kennedy, I really don't know where to start. First, I am sorry for the short notice, but this was the only place that I felt that it was right to come."

"You are fine Tonya. I take it that this isn't about you being ready to come back to work, is it?"

She shook her head no and the tears began to roll. "I fucked up. We fucked up," she wept.

"Tonya, are you saying what I think you're saying right now?"

She looked up at me and shook her head yes. "I am so sorry Kingston. I didn't mean for this to happen. I promise, you won't have any issues. I just had to come let you know. I got the DNA results back in the mail and this isn't his baby. You are the only other man that I've ever been with."

My heart fell into the bottom of my seat. I couldn't breathe. My hands began to shake and I felt a warmness come over my body.

"Again, I am so sorry. I didn't mean for any of this to happen. I never expected my drama to interfere with your life. What we had meant nothing. It was an honest mistake, to tell the truth."

I stopped her before she said another word. "Does he know?"

She took a deep breath and began to weep harder. She shook her head no. It was a bit of a relief that he didn't at the moment; I knew that eventually he would find out but, by that time, things would have calmed down. My life was on fire now and slowly beginning to choke me with its flames.

"I'm not going to tell him. I don't want him to feel like I've betrayed his trust. He is a good man and you should see the way that he treats this child. He loves him with everything in his being. I cannot destroy that. I simply came to inform you that this is your son and I wanted to give you a chance to say both hello and goodbye."

"Tonya, what the hell are you talking about?"

"Kingston, let's be honest for a moment. I don't have a chance with you. What we shared was simply a moment of lust that was amazing but wrong. We both have situations and one of us has more secrets than they have time. I don't want to be entangled into that web. I have decided not to come back to work for you because it would be too much of a strain on me both mentally and emotionally, knowing that my child's father would really not be his father. I feel like such a cheap hoe right now."

I got up from my seat and walked over to her. I wiped the tears from her eyes. I swallowed a fair amount of the saliva that formed in my mouth and placed one of my hands on my head.

"A part of me wants to tell you that there is no way in hell that I won't be a part of my child's life, but the other part understands exactly where you are coming from. I agree with your decision to keep Eric in the dark about this and make sure that the baby has a man in his life that will love and cherish him. As much as I want you back here working for me, I understand your stance on that as well. I can only hope that, as time goes on, those feelings change. The door will always be open for you here." I took my hand and placed it on her chin, lifting her face. "If there ever comes a time where my child wants to know the truth, you have him come find me. I don't want him feeling like he's not worth anything because he's being raised by another man. We may not know one another anymore than the time spent in this office, but I want you to know that you nor he will ever have an issue in this world, as long as there is blood pumping through my veins. If you need a single penny for him, you let me know. I will make provisions to see that you are accommodated."

Her water works began to run again. I kneeled and looked at the baby in the seat and saw myself. I took him out of the seat and held him in my arms for a moment. Kissing his forehead, I looked over at her and asked his name.

"His name is Kaizer."

I looked at him and smiled. "Kaizer. I like that. Make sure you take care of your mother, man. I'll see you in a few years." I kissed his forehead and placed him back in his seat."

With my attention back on Tonya, I wiped her tears once more. I pulled her close and hugged her. "Everything's going to be ok. We made this bed, we just have to lay in it."

As we stood in my office intertwined in a hug, India walked back through the doors. The hug ended and the two of us backed away from one another.

"Uhhhh. What the hell going on in here? Everything ok? Y'all got something y'all need to tell me?"

"No, India. She was just telling me that she decided not to come back to work for me. Her and her husband decided that it would be best if she just stayed home and raised the baby."

India looked towards Tonya and her emotions shifted. "I thought you were trying to steal my man. Hell, with the way y'all was hugged up, I almost thought that you was telling him that lil man was his. What's his name anyway?" India questioned as she reached in and gave her a farewell hug of her own.

"It's Kai-"

I interrupted and spoke up for her. "His name is Cap."

Tonya looked at me with a side eye but understood that I was throwing her as far off as completely possible. If she got wind of the K in the child's name, her assumption may be more of a reality than she expected.

"Well Tonya, Cap is beautiful. I pray that he grows to be big, tall, and successful just like his father. We should have a play date when he gets older. Please don't be a stranger, we love you, and if you know of any good secretaries, please send them this way. Kingston must get rid of that one out there. I don't like her. She young and stupid. She looks like the type that'll get in her feelings and try to fuck my man. I can't have that. I might have to tap some ass."

Tonya looked in my direction, then gave the most heartfelt fuck you smile to India. She grabbed the baby's car seat and headed out the door. Just like that, a chapter was opened and closed in my life. One fire down, a thousand more to go.

I looked at India and she at me.

"Well, let's go. I'm still hungry and you don't have an appointment any more. Let's go spend some quality time before I change my mind."

I grabbed my things and the two of us headed down towards the car. In the back of my mind, I felt like this situation was far from over. I knew that it wasn't near over. It was just one more piece to the puzzle that had to be fixed.

My biggest question was how to break this shit down to Tahleea. I needed to hear from her, ASAP.

Chapter 7

India

"So, what you got a taste for handsome?" I asked Kingston as we made our way towards my car. When we approached it, he opened the driver's door for me and let me in. Once closing me inside, he walked around to the passenger side and hopped in.

"Whatever you decide baby, I'm just along for the time to spend with you," he replied, buckling his seat belt.

"Aww, give me a kiss!" I chirped, leaning over and planting a juicy one onto his lips. "I have a taste for some good Mexican food. I don't know why, but I've been craving enchiladas," I continued. Kingston looked at me with a side eye. He then plastered a sly grin upon his face.

"What? Why are you looking at me like that?" I asked curiously.

"Because you know exactly why you're craving enchiladas. I know why you're craving them; you're just still in denial," he stated, shaking his head. I immediately smacked my lips and waved him off.

"Oh gawd! Here you go with this shit again," I spat as I fastened my seat belt, cranked the engine, and commenced to pulling out of the parking lot of his office building. "I keep telling you that I'm not pregnant Kingston!" I hissed.

"Okay, so why you won't just take a test and prove me wrong then? Shut me up if it's not true," he told me. I took a deep frustrated breath and cut my eyes at him.

"Fine! Fine, Kingston. When you get home from work, I will have a test and I will take it for you! Okay!" I snapped.

"Cool, but why you gotta get so upset?" he asked.

"I'm not upset. I'm just sick of you saying that I'm pregnant and I keep telling you that I'm not. It's like you don't want to take my word for it. Like I told you before, I know my body and I would know if I were pregnant," I continued.

"Okay, well you said you will pee on a stick, so we'll let the test confirm that," he stated while leaning his head back against the headrest, deading the conversation. I simply rolled my eyes at him and cursed him under my breath. He was becoming real adamant about me taking a pregnancy test and it was starting to piss me off. I had to think of a way around it, at least until I made my mind up about what I was going to do. A part of me couldn't just kill an innocent child that didn't ask to be made, but I would've been a dumb bitch to keep it and leave my husband for a nigga like Memphis. Yea, he was talking a good game about how he would take care of us and how we would have no worries, but that's all it was, talk. At the end of the day, he still had Tahleea and they were still married. He could talk all about how much he didn't want her until his face turned blue, but there was no telling what he was saying when he went back home to her. I couldn't just base my decisions off words; Memphis was going to have to show and prove.

The rest of our car ride was pure silence. After about ten minutes, I pulled up to a Mexican restaurant called El Borracho, and we got out and headed in. Upon entry, we were greeted by a short, elderly Mexican hostess.

"Table for two please," I stated, and she showed us to our seats. After placing our menus in front of us, she took our drink orders and left us alone to decide on our food.

"What you plan in ordering babe?" I asked, breaking the awkward silence.

"I think I'm going to just order me a couple of soft tacos; I'm really not that hungry," he replied, closing his menu. I already knew what I wanted, so there was no need for me to even look. When the waitress came back with our drinks, we placed our order. She repeated what we ordered, took our menus, and left us alone once more.

"So, honey, I was thinking, we should get KJ into some karate classes or something. When I took him to school this morning, they had a lil flyer hanging up promoting karate tutorials. I thought that would be fun for him," I stated, sparking a conversation.

"Aw, hell nah! You ain't bout to have his lil bad ass running around Judo chopping me in my neck and shin!" Kingston blurted out, and I damn near choked up on my sweet tea from laughing at his silly ass.

"Really bae?" I asked, still giggling hard as hell.

"Yea, really. His bad ass already think he a power ranger that got super powers. His ass learn some karate, he really gon lose his mind." He laughed. I couldn't even do anything but laugh with him. He was being honest; KJ stayed running around playing out the things that he'd seen on tv. My baby was so smart and full of energy.

"But nah, for real, I think it's a good idea. I think he would enjoy that." Kingston got serious. "What we need to do to get him in?" he asked.

"Well, I got the flyer; I'll just call later to see what we need to do," I told him.

"Okay cool, let me know," he replied. We chit chatted a little more and, before we knew it, the waitress was back with our food. She sat the sizzling plates in front of us and asked if we needed anything else. After confirming that we were good, she left us me to enjoy our meal. Grabbing

Kingston's hands, we said grace and proceeded to dig in. Two bites into my enchiladas, I felt myself getting nauseous. Cupping my hand over my mouth, I began to gag.

"Damn baby, you iight?" Kingston asked, immediately taking notice. I quickly shook my head, grabbed a napkin, and spat in it.

"Yea, I'm fine. I think I ate a pepper." I lied, then proceeded to try to keep eating. In the midst, my phone began to ring and Tahleea's name popped up. Kingston's eyes wandered to my screen, then back up at me. I didn't want to interrupt our date, so I decided to let it ring and I would hit her up later. As I continued to scoff down my food, my stomach began to get weaker and weaker. At the same time I began to gag again, Tahleea began to call once more.

"Excuse me babe, I'll be right back," I said, quickly snatching my phone from the table and running off to the ladies' room. When I got in there, I busted into the closest stall and began barfing. I let out everything that would come up, then flushed the toilet. Going to the sink, I grabbed a paper towel, wet it with cool water, and began wiping my face. I then rinsed the nasty throw-up taste from my mouth and patted it dry. After washing and drying my hands, I went to call Tahleea back but, as soon as I was about to press her contact, she was calling me back. It was unlikely for her to blow me up the way she was, so I immediately answered.

"Hey girl, what's up?" I spoke into my cell.

"Damn baby, a nigga gotta blow you up to get you to answer the phone?" Memphis replied, throwing me all the way off.

"Memphis?"

"Nah, Dallas! Yea, this Memphis, what took you so long to pick up?" he asked.

"I'm out to lunch with Kingston, and why the hell are you calling me from Tahleea's phone!? Are you out of your mind? What are you trying to do, get us caught the fuck up?" I hissed. I didn't know what was running through that sick ass head of his, but he was playing with fire by calling me from his wife's phone, knowing that we kept in touch.

"Man chill, she not even here. But look, man, I need you to do me a favor. I really need you to come through for the kid though," he stated.

"Oh gawd! What is it Memphis?" I asked frustrated, while rolling my eyes to the top of my head.

"I need a loan. All of my money is tied up into this business deal I got going and I dun ran up on a sticky situation. I promise to pay you every cent back soon, like in the next couple of weeks," he stated. I released a deep sigh. His ass was just telling me how he was going to take care of me and this baby and, yet, he was already asking me for fucking money. Where they do that at?

"How much Memphis?" I asked, biting the inside of my jaw.

"Fifty thousand!" he said like it was nothing.

"What?! Fifty grand? You must be out of your fuckin mind! Where am I suppose to get that kind of money without raising Kingston's brow? No, no, I can't do it!" I shot.

"Come on ma, I need you! I know you can get the money without him knowing. Between you and that nigga, I know for a fact y'all loaded with cash. I just need this one solid; I promise, I will never ask for anything else. I'll have the money back in two weeks or less, my word," he pleaded.

"Why can't you ask your wife? I know she has it!" I shot.

"Come on now, baby; now why would I ask her for anything when I'm tryna leave her to be with you?" he said smoothly. I sat quiet for a second as I pondered on my decision.

"Two weeks Memphis! You got two weeks to give me my money back, not a second later!" I told him.

"My muthafuckn girl! I swear I love yo ass!" he chirped.

"Yea, yea! Call me later; I need to get back to Kingston," I told him.

"Iight baby, bet!" he said before ending the call. Shaking my head, I took a deep breath and headed back to the table to rejoin my husband.

"Is everything alright babe?" he asked when I sat back down.

"Yea, everything's fine. I was just talking to Tahleea. She wants to get together for another girl's day!" I lied. Kingston shook his head as he continued eating his tacos. It was only a matter of time before my lies would soon catch up to me.

Chapter 8

Kingston

The lunch date between India and I had drawn to an end. The ride back to my office was awkwardly silent. There were several things consuming my thoughts as I looked out of the window, watching the city blur by. As we pulled up to my office to part ways, I looked over at her, trying to find the words to speak. No words ever came. I got out of the car and began to walk towards the door of my building when she rolled her window down and called out for me.

"Kingston!"

I turned to look back at her as she threw her head back, motioning me to return to the car. I patted my pockets, ensuring that I didn't leave anything, then walked back over to her.

"What's up?"

She grabbed my tie and pulled my face down into the opening of the window. "I just wanted to tell you that I love you. Thanks for having lunch with me. I'll see you when you get home."

She released my tie and rolled the window back up. I stood in place, watching the tail lights of her car slowly creep away. I took a deep breath and pulled my phone out. I was hoping to see a text from Tahleea, but I had nothing but the time and a few unread emails on my home screen. It was unlike her to not let me know that she had her phone back but, nonetheless, I tried not to let it shake me. I entered the building and took the elevator up to my office floor.

Upon my entrance into my office, I noticed that there was a gentleman sitting in the chair across from my desk with his feet propped up on the top of it.

"Excuse me, can I help you?"

I must have startled him because he quickly turned towards me and placed his hand on his waist line. When he looked up, he immediately took a sigh of relief.

"Got damn Kingston, man. You moving like a fucking assassin in this motherfucker. Ring a bell or something next time."

"You reach for your waist again, you gone feel an assassin. What the fuck are you doing in my office, Hitman?"

He stood to his feet and shook my hand, as I approached both our desk.

"I'm just here on business man. You know that's the only reason I could be here. I'm trying to make sure we good."

I knew what he was eluding to, but I wanted to make him sweat a bit before I gave him any information. "What do you mean are we good?" I asked obnoxiously.

"Come on Kingston. I've watched you build an empire from a corner stone. We got too much history for you to be playing with me. I'd hate to see all this shit crumble beneath you."

I looked at him with a devious grin. "Was that a threat sir?"

"You can take it how you want to. I ain't trying to go to war with you, Kingston, but trust me when I say whenever I feel like pulling the plug, I can end all of this shit for you."

I continued to look at Hitman. I knew the type of shit he was capable of, but he also knew what I was capable of. Although I had placed that part of my life in the rearview, I was sure he knew that I was still a very dangerous threat. "Let not go to war then, Hitman. You here on business, so let's talk business."

"That's more like it", he stated, sitting back in his seat.

"I've got you cut into a new deal I've worked. You'll be able to survive off the interest alone and remain a partial minority owner.

"My nigga. I knew I could count on you. I do have one question for you."

I looked up at him as he cut me off in mid-sentence. "What is it?"

"I hate to ask, especially since you done pretty much put me on, my nigga, but you still got that money?"

"What money?" I replied.

"What money? Real funny Kingston. You know what money I'm talking about. I need a loan from it."

This nigga must have lost all his damn marbles if he thought he was getting a penny from me. I looked at him and my wheels began to turn. "I'm serious my nigga, what money?"

He looked into my eyes and smirked. "Aight Kingston." He placed his hands on the arms of his seat and stood to his feet. "I just needed some help bruh. I got into some shit and needed a quick little bail out, but I understand that you can't help me. Just keep this in mind when you need some work done and want to keep ya hands clean."

I sat back in my chair and propped my feet up on it. I didn't say a word; I just pointed to the door with a pen, informing him that he could leave. That was the second threat from him in a matter of minutes. One thing that I refused to tolerate was disrespect and he was showing it in its purest form.

As he made his way to the door, he made a statement that was rather peculiar. "Watch that bitch of yours, my nigga." Then, the door slammed behind him.

I mouthed the words to myself, attempting to understand where they came from. The more I thought on it, the deeper my thoughts ran. He didn't know anything about my personal life at home, so his statement may have just been words formed from anger. Nonetheless, I brushed it off and returned my focus to my work. I picked my phone up momentarily, still anticipating a text from Tahleea and, yet, there remained not even one.

My work day had come to an end and the words from Hitman's lips began to ring like an alarm in the back of my head. It wasn't like Tahleea to not reach out to me, especially after reaching out to India. After our last interaction with one another, I was almost for certain that their friendship would almost be nonexistent. Hell, I didn't want to do business with her husband, due to the fact that her and I were making plans to be with one another. She was certainly moving in a manner that I didn't see coming, nor was I ok with it. Instead of going directly home, I made a quick detour past her shop to see if I could catch her there before she headed home for the evening.

As I approached the street in which her shop was on, I noticed her car in the parking lot. I parked across the street in front of another business and dialed the number on the front of her shop's door.

"Hello?" I heard her assistant Dana answer.

"What's up Dana? Is Tahleea in?"

"Who is this?"

"It's Mr. Kennedy. Is she in?"

I heard Dana whispering in the background to someone.

"Give me one second Mr. Kennedy."

She handed the phone off to Tahleea and the two of them had an exchange, trying to figure out who I was.

"Hello," Tahleea answered.

"Well, got damn, hello stranger. How are you this evening?"

"Kingston… why are you calling the shop phone? Is everything ok?"

I looked at her through the glass of her shop, debating on whether I should get out and go speak. "Everything is fine on my end. Are you ok is the question? I haven't heard from you."

She paused for a moment before she answered. "Yes, everything is fine. Where are you?"

I blew my horn and her head popped up. She noticed me sitting across the street and waved.

"What are you doing crazy ass man. You know this nigga likes to creep around the area. Are you trying to get us caught up?"

"I'm not worried about that nigga in the least bit. Yo ass is mine. Besides, you sitting here calling my wife and can't pick up the phone to send a text and say hello. What kind of shit is that?"

A very awkward silence buzzed across the phone before she broke it. "Kingston, what the hell are you talking about. You know that I gave Memphis my phone. How the hell would I call you?"

In that instance, I felt hell cover my body. Either Tahleea was playing me for a fool or India knew more than one motherfucker named Tahleea. For the moment, I was following my first mind because there was no way in hell that there was another person in the world with such a unique name.

"Hello," she spoke into the phone.

I cleared my throat and got back to the conversation. "Yeah, I'm here. I just wanted to hear your voice for a moment. Hopefully, we can get together soon. We've got some shit to discuss. In the meantime, figure out how to get that phone back. I can't have too many more days without talking to you. So, handle that for me. I'll be in touch."

I disconnected the call and put my car in drive, pulling off in a hurry. I was pissed. With everything that we'd been through and were trying to start together, Tahleea just lied to me without any remorse. It left a bad taste in my mouth, but there was still a slight chance that she was being truthful. It was just a matter of time before I knew that answer.

I got home with hell still draped all over me.

"DADDY!" KJ exclaimed as I walked through the door.

I bent over and picked him up. I gave him a warm hug and kissed his forehead. I put him back on the floor and took my suit coat off, placing it on the coat rack by the front door.

"KJ, where's mommy?"

He pointed towards our bedroom and I took a deep breath. Before I headed towards its direction, I sent him to his room to watch some cartoons. I proceeded to walk into the kitchen and pour me a glass of the closest thing available. I felt myself building on an already bad situation and I wanted to try to calm my nerves so that India didn't see the discontent on my face.

I walked into the bedroom and noticed her laughing on the phone, as she laid across the bed. I began to unbutton my shirt and sat my glass on my nightstand. I looked over at her, as she was coming to the end of her conversation.

"OK girl, I will talk to you later. Love you too." She turned her attention towards me and gave off a slight smirk. "Well, hello there Mr. How was the rest of your day at work?"

"It was fine. How was your day?"

"It's been fine. I been waiting on you to get here so that I can go ahead and prove you wrong about this pregnancy shit you keep trying to cast upon me. Where's the test?"

I took a deep breath. In my rage, I had completely forgot to stop and grab a test. It honestly was the last thing on my mind. "I'll have to grab one tomorrow. I completely forgot."

"Shame on you, Mr. Kennedy. It's ok. Work must have kicked your ass. Come here and let mama rub the stress away."

She crawled over behind me and propped herself up on her knees. She began to rub my shoulders and kiss my neck. "So, what's on your mind?" she whispered in my ear.

I reached over to the nightstand and grabbed my glass. I took a couple sips and began to release my thoughts.

"I honestly don't know where to start. It's been one hell of a day. I guess the day itself wasn't too bad, it's just been some actions by others. Can I ask you a question and will you be completely honest with me?"

"What is it baby?"

"Would you ever lie to me to preserve my feelings. It could be the simplest of shit, would you?"

She started to giggle and began to work her hands a little harder over my shoulders. "Besides telling you that you haven't gained a little weight, I don't think that I could baby. Why do you ask?"

"I was just curious. No reason in particular." I took another sip from my glass and placed it back on the night stand. I allowed her hands to do their job and put me at ease. "Hey, have you heard from Tahleea lately? I been trying to get in touch with Memphis lately, but can't seem to get in touch with him."

She stopped the massage, and I could feel her palms instantly become clammy.

"You aight?" I asked.

"Yeah, I'm fine baby. I'm sorry. I was just trying to wipe my hands off. Your skin is really warm."

"Oh, ok. Well, have you?"

"I have. That was her that I was on the phone with as you walked in. I heard the alarm chime, so I figured you were home so I began to wrap the conversation up. As far as Memphis, she told me that he lost his phone, so he's been hard to reach. If I talk to her again tomorrow, I will relay the message, if that's ok with you."

"No, it's ok baby. No need to do that. I'm sure he will have another phone before the week is out. I'll just wait for him to reach out to me."

"Speaking of Tahleea, though. I kind of fucked up and said yes to something that she asked me. I hope you don't get mad, but she needed to borrow some money to take care of a debt, but she is going to pay it back to me in the next two weeks."

"How much money we talking India?"

"It's really not that much. I checked the accounts before I said yes."

"How much?"

"Fifty thousand."

I couldn't believe what I had just heard. I turned my head and cut my eyes at India. It was never in her nature to allow anyone to borrow anything. Now, suddenly, she and Tahleea had become best friends and she's giving out loans. Something wasn't adding up with either one of them and I was getting to the bottom of this so-called friendship of theirs if it killed me. In the back of my mind, it was time to start eliminating motherfuckers from this equation, starting with Tahleea.

I grabbed my phone and looked at the clock on it. It was late enough for Tahleea to be home, so I excused myself from the room. I went into the bathroom and began to prep my shower but, before I could, I sent her a text.

We need to talk. I got some shit that's been bothering me and I need to discuss it with you in person. So, I will see you at the shop in the am. -KINGSTON

With the text showing that it had been sent and delivered, I stared at myself in the brightly lit mirror before me. I saw the side of me that I thought I had left in the past beginning to surface and he was ready to cause hell.

Chapter 9

Tahleea

I pulled into the driveway of my home and placed my car into park. Taking a deep sigh of relief, I was happy to see that Memphis' car was gone. After a long day at the shop of sewing and taking dress orders, I wanted to do nothing but take a long hot shower and climb into my bed. On top of that, I was still thinking about how Kingston called up to my shop, accusing me of calling and making plans with his wife. I didn't know why he didn't believe me, but I had never and would never lie to him about anything. I didn't get to get my phone back from Memphis and give him the one I bought him because when I made it home earlier that morning, he was already gone. I had to make it to the shop, so I didn't stick around to wait for him. I honestly didn't know what Kingston was talking about, but I was sure in the hell going to find out.

Shutting off my ignition, I grabbed my Birkin bag from the passenger seat and hopped out. Making my way to the front door, I unlocked it and let myself in. The house was pitch black dark, so I sat my purse down on my China table next to the door, while I felt my way around for a light switch. Scaring the shit out of me, Memphis flicked the lights on before I could.

"Aw, so you finally decided to bring yo hoe ass home?" he stated with a menacing stare.

"Uhm, what are you talking about Memphis? I've been home," I shot back.

"Yea, you came home to get ready for work, but you ain't bring yo ass home after sneaking yo ass up out of here last night!" he seethed.

"I didn't sneak out; I just didn't want to wake you. And I did come home, I just got in late. Maybe you would've known that if you wouldn't have drunk that whole fifth of Hennessy last night before passing out!" I lied. When I came home earlier, I noticed an empty bottle by the sofa with a blanket and I immediately knew he had been drinking, so I used that to play on his intelligence. "I left before you woke up. I went to Sprint to get you a new phone; when I came back, you were gone. I didn't have time to stick around because I had to be at the shop, so I left the phone on the bed," I continued. Memphis stood there sucking his teeth, looking me square in the face as if he knew I were lying. My heart began to pound frivolously as I anticipated what would come next.

"So, where you go last night?" he asked calmly.

"I just went to Dana's. She picked me up and we went to her house and had a little girl's night with just us two. We sipped wine, cooked, listened to music; you know, girl stuff," I lied again. Memphis began to crack his knuckles and pop his neck. I immediately began to ease back away from him, in case he decided to swing, but it didn't help. Swiftly snatching me up by my collar, Memphis threw me into our living room wall, making pictures fall on top of my head. Tears immediately began to fall from my eyes as my head began to pound from the pain.

"You must think I'm some dumb nigga, huh?!" he said while clenching tighter onto throat, closing my wind pipe. I began to try and shake my head no, as I clawed at his hands to release me. He then shoved his hand up my dress and stuck his fingers inside of me. He pulled them out and smelled them. After not smelling anything, he let my throat loose. I began to pant and cough as I gasped for air, trying to catch my breath. "Let me find out you out here fuckin around on me and I swear for God, I'ma kill yo ass!" he seethed. His sick ass then stuck his fingers into his mouth and sucked them.

"Mmm damn, that pussy taste good! I would suck that muthafucka, but I got shit to do," he said, grinning. I wished so bad that Kingston had just busted a fat nut inside of me, so he would've be tasting his semen. I cut my eyes at him as I continued to rub my throat, trying to soothe it. He then tossed me my phone.

"Here, call that slut ass, ghetto assistant of yours. Apparently, she needs to talk to you; she sent you a urgent message," he said, turning to leave the house. He then did an about face and walked back over to me.

"My bad, thanks for the phone baby." He kissed me on the forehead and left. I immediately went to the message he was referring to and read it. After taking in the context and looking at the number, I knew it was Kingston and quickly texted back.

Just got my phone back baby. Call me when you can. -Tahleea

In no time, he replied.

Can't talk right now but I need you to meet me at our spot ASAP! It's a lot of shit that's not sitting right with me and I need to see you soon. -Kingston

Reading the message, I began to get confused because I couldn't figure out what was wrong.

Okay, just let me know when. -Tahleea

I just simply texted back. I guessed I would find out sooner or later what the hell was on his mind. Making my way up the stairs, I prepared myself for a shower; after that, it was bedtime for me.

Chapter 10

Memphis

"Got damn, I wish this bitch would answer the phone," I stated out loud to myself as I sat in my car calling India.

"You've reached Mrs. Kennedy, leave a message after the beep."

"Aye man, I need you to answer yo phone. I need to talk to you about that money. Call me."

I didn't bother to leave who I was on the voicemail. The bitch had better know my voice. I sparked a blunt and began to play with the new phone Tahleea brought home to me. I remained in the driveway for a minute, trying to download as much of my information as I could from the ICloud to the phone. I had several contacts, as well as important notes saved and backed up, just in case I ever ran into a situation like this.

I looked up into the bedroom window where Tahleea was undressing. Watching her as she moved about the room, I noticed her answering her phone. I watched Tahleea move around the room. Tahleea must have thought I was a fool. I been in this game far too long to believe that her ass been out all night and not fucked around. Game recognize game and the move she just made was far too familiar. Her pussy didn't have a scent, which meant that she cleaned herself up before she got home. Nonetheless, it was time better spent not arguing or beating her ass. She was granted her moment for now. I had bigger shit to tend to.

I started the engine and backed out of the driveway with Lucci blasting through the speakers. Before I could turn the corner, my phone began to buzz. It was India.

Hey, I got your message. I can't talk right now, he is right here next to me. Just text me. -India

I read over the message and shook my head. I needed to hear her voice and wasn't taking no for an answer.

Fuck that nigga. Call me now. -Memphis

I just told you I can't. Text me. -India

You don't tell me what you can and can't do. I told you to call me and that's what needs to happen now. Don't forget you carrying my baby, not his. Now, get yo ass up, go in another room, and call me. -Memphis

It took a couple minutes, but my point got across to her. I looked down at my phone and her number was displayed. "I figured you'd see shit my way. What's up?"

"What Memphis? I told you I couldn't talk so make it fast."

I chuckled for a moment, then returned my focus to the conversation. "What, you ain't got time for yo nigga? Fuck Kingston square ass. I'm just trying to check on my baby."

"Are you fucking serious right now?"

"On top of other things, yeah, I am. Is that an issue."

She got quiet on the other end of the phone before I heard her yell out. "I'm just using the bathroom KJ. I'll be out in a minute baby… hello."

"Yeah, I'm still here."

"Look Memphis, I ain't about to play this game with you. I told you I couldn't talk right now. I got shit to do."

"I understand you a busy woman but, on a serious note, was you able to handle that for me?"

She got silent again, then took a deep breath. "Yes Memphis, it's handled. I need this shit back in two week. I don't want to have to come find you."

"You ain't got to worry about that, I got you. In the meantime, I like the way that sound, you cumming for me and all."

"I'm not fucking with you right now. Is that it? I have to go."

"That's it, just hit me tomorrow so we can link up and I can get that from you."

I heard a knock at the door and Kingston talking in the faint distant.

"India, you ok in there?"

"Yes, I'm fine Kingston. I'll be out in a minute. Aight, KJ getting, anxious hurry up."

"Shit, I got to go Memphis. I'll call you in the morning," she whispered into the phone right before it disconnected.

I took a sigh of relief and deeply inhaled my blunt. It was a weight off my shoulders to have a little bread back in my pocket. I had to figure out how to finesse this nigga, Hitman. Now that I knew the money was secured, I had to work my magic and do what I thought was best. I found his number in the contact list and placed a call to him.

"Who dis?" he answered after the second ring.

"It's yo hero, nigga. Christmas came early for yo punk ass. I'll have something for you tomorrow."

"Who the fuck is this and what you mean you'll have something for me?"

"Nigga, it's Memphis. Relax. I couldn't pull the whole boat, but I got you half way there."

"Oh, what's up fuu and what you mean half the boat? I done already told these folks that I would have all of it. You gave me yo word that I would have all of it."

"I know what I said man, but either you gone take it or leave it. I did what I could."

Hitman grew silent for a moment. I could tell that it wasn't the answer that he was looking for. He cleared his throat then spoke.

"Aight, man, just meet me at yo studio. At least if I take that to them, I can buy myself a little bit more time. You killing me, my nigga."

"How you think I feel pulling this shit off for you. All that matters is that I got it. I'll meet you there in the morning. Just call me when you're on your way."

The call disconnected and I took another hit of my blunt. The truth of the matter was that I didn't have any intentions on giving him fifty grand. He was lucky to be getting the half that I was putting up for him. I needed to make a few plays and flip the money to benefit myself. There was still some shit that I wanted to do with it and, now that I knew that it was secured, I was going to have my way.

Chapter 11

Kingston

The time came for me to meet up with Tahleea. I sat in the room with the lights off, waiting for her to arrive. Looking around at the four walls, I began to reminisce on everything she and I had gone through in this one small, secluded area. We explored so much with one another; it held so many of our pains, secrets, and lustful adventures. I looked at the sheets on the bed and, although they may have not been the same exact sheets she wrapped herself in, it reminded me of when she was at her weakest and bore her soul to me. She let me see her for who she truly was, and I accepted her flaws and all. As that thought alone ran laps around my mind, it didn't make things any easier for the conversation to come.

A bright glare came through the window of the room and I walked over to see if it was her. To my pleasure, it was. I went to the door and opened it, anticipating for her to walk through it. She greeted me with a hug as she entered.

"What up baby. I missed you," she spoke as she wrapped her arms around my neck and kissed me gently.

"I missed you too. Come on in here."

I looked around the outside of the room to make sure that no one had followed her. Although this was our little spot, I was cautious of everything. She noticed my suspicious nature and spoke on it.

"Everything ok? You acting real weird."

"Yeah, everything is fine," I answered.

"Kingston... come on now, I know you. What the hell is going on?"

I wasted no time gathering my thoughts; before I knew it, I had released my frustrations.

"You tell me, Tahleea. I thought we were better than going behind one another's back. I'm trying to build some shit with you and, yet, you and my fucking wife are acting like y'all are sister wives. If you needed something, why didn't you come to me?"

She looked at me with a side eye and took a deep breath. "Excuse me?"

"Come on now, Tahleea; if you were strapped for cash, why didn't you just come to me?"

She rolled her eyes and made a motion, grabbing towards her chest as if she was in disbelief.

"India told me that you ran into a situation and you needed to borrow some money from her. It didn't make sense to me then and it doesn't now. If you needed something, you know I would have did that for you."

"Whoa… Kingston… ok." She gathered her thoughts and shook her head as if she had been hit with a ton of bricks. "Kingston, I don't know what the fuck you and that bitch you call a wife of yours are trying to pull, but I don't need your money. I'm not hurting for anything. I don't know where she would get that idea, but that's not me. I'll be damned if I ask another bitch for anything. Besides, I haven't talked to India in a while."

I took a step back and placed my hand on my head. I began scratching my scalp, confused about everything.

"What do you mean you haven't talked to India? You were on the phone with her the other day when I came home. That's when she told me that you needed to borrow some money."

"Kingston, if you recall, I gave my phone to Memphis. I haven't talked to that woman."

I remained puzzled as I turned away from her, trying to piece it all together. *Why the fuck would India lie to me?* I pondered to myself.

"I don't know why the pregnant bitch is deciding to bring me into whatever bullshit that y'all have going on, but I'm not with that shit. I especially don't appreciate you coming at me like this either about it."

"What a minute… she isn't pregnant… is she?"

"Kingston, you have got to be shitting me. She still hasn't told you? She been pregnant for a while; hell, she was supposed to tell you the day she and I went out to the spa. It took everything in me not to blow up and whoop her ass. That's all she kept talking about is being pregnant with your got damn baby. I wanted to just call you then and end this situation, but I thought better of myself and you, so I just let the shit slide."

I felt the weight of the world weighing me down. I walked over and sat on the bed next to her and processed the news she just broke to me. I could barely breathe but, in a way, I was relieved to know that I wasn't crazy about her pregnancy.

"You really didn't know, huh? That's typical. You need to watch that bitch, baby. I know what we doing is wrong but, if she wouldn't tell the man that she is so in love with that she was pregnant, she is hiding something."

I dropped my head to the floor. The whole baby situation brought me back to one of the reasons that we were in the hotel room. I placed my hand on her thigh and began to apologize.

"I'm sorry."

"Don't be sorry Kingston, you didn't know. I accept your apology, but you can't spazz out on me like that. I don't know who ya bitch talking to, but it damn sure ain't me, baby."

She leaned over and hugged me. I embraced her, then pushed her away for a moment. "I have something that I need to tell you. Although what we are doing is wrong, it feels right and there isn't anything that I want to hide from you moving forward."

She pushed her body away from me and looked into my eyes. I could tell that she was preparing her head for the worse. "Kingston, I don't like the way that sounds or the way that you are looking at me. Just tell me."

"I've fathered another baby outside of my marriage."

She grew quiet. Her eyes became blood red. "You did what Kingston? What the fuck you mean fathered another child? So, the little motherfucker is already born? Hello?" she questioned, snapping her fingers.

I was hesitant to repeat myself and, just as I formed my lips to speak, she stopped me.

"Don't fix yo lips to say it again. I hope that was a motherfucking joke Kingston. I really pray that you were just kidding."

I shook my head no and I saw the tears rolling down her face. "It was in the heat of the moment and it just happened."

"So, who is the lucky bitch? As a matter of fact, don't answer that either; it doesn't matter. The bigger question is how the fuck does you fucking a bitch just happen? That makes no fucking sense. You catching a flat tire, just happens. You falling off a bike, just happens. Yo dick is way too big for it just to fall in a bitch, nut, and say it just happens Kingston. I know you. I know how you like to fuck. So, do you want to come correct this time with a reasonable answer?"

She stood to her feet and grabbed both her wristlet and keys while looking at me, as she backed herself towards the door.

"Baby, where are you going?" I asked as I stood to my feet, reaching for her arm.

"Don't fucking touch me. I can't believe you. I'm sitting here being a faithful side bitch, waiting for us to have our chance, and you fucking up. I ain't even made it into the main bitch's position yet and you already fucking me over. You ain't no better than the nigga that I'm married to."

I reached for her once more, attempting to plead my case, but she wasn't having any parts of it. She turned her body towards me and, in the blink of an eye, she left an impression of her hand upon my face.

"I loved you, Kingston. I would have done anything in this world for you, and this is how you do me? I go above and beyond to make sure that I do things right by you and I still get fucked. I could see if I was the bitch you got at home that don't take care of your needs, let you tell it. From the looks of things, I guess that was a lie too. I'm out man. Don't call me, I'll call you if or when I need you. Have a good life Kingston."

I stood with my hand applied to my face, nursing the sensation that she left on it. Just like that, she was gone. She never heard me out, never gave me a chance to explain. She was just gone.

I sat back onto the bed, dropping my head into my hands. So many thoughts and questions surrounded me. How could India go and tell someone else that she was pregnant but continue to lie to me? Who the fuck could she have been talking to if it wasn't Tahleea about the money? My wife had become someone I didn't know, and we were in the same house. Her dishonesty put a damper on my trust with Tahleea. Although I knew that she had no reason to lie to me, her knowing about the pregnancy and not saying anything until now didn't sit well however. Nevertheless, I knew that I couldn't stay on the bed for the rest of my life. I had to get up and get back to reality. Just as I got up to leave, reality struck in the form of Hitman calling my phone.

Chapter 12

Tahleea

I walked out of the hotel room confused and pissed as hell. It was taking everything in me not to turn around, go back in, and stab Kingston the fuck up with my pocket knife. Out of all the people, how could he do this to me? He knew everything that I had been going through. He was there at my lowest of the low. I shared everything with him; and he had the audacity to accuse me of being a liar, then turn around and tell me he was the father of another woman's baby. He had me so fucked up. He knew how bad I wanted to be a mother and how hard I struggled to carry a baby. It was like a spit in my face, and I was so disgusted. Kingston was supposed to be my protector, my confidante, my best friend, and now I didn't even know him anymore.

Hopping into my car, I immediately broke down. Throwing my purse against the passenger door window, everything began to fall out of it. I banged my fist against the steering wheel as I cried and screamed out in agony. My heart hurt so bad that it felt as if I was about to die. *I trusted you, I trusted you, why would you do this to meeeee!* I screamed as I continued to cry and beat up the steering wheel. I was so abashed that I didn't know what to do next. The person who told me to trust him had betrayed me in the worst way. I should've known better than to trust a nigga who cheated on his wife anyway; it was only a matter of time before he would do it to me. Kingston had no loyalty to his wife, so why would I expect him to have any towards me? He was just the typical nigga who tried to catch a nut from any woman with titties and ass, and there my gullible ass was thinking he was different. It was cool though because he had lost the best thing that had ever happened to him. He and his disloyal ass, sneaky ass, lying ass wife could have each other and burn in the fire pits of hell for all I cared. I was done! I had a husband at home who abused me physically; I be dammed if I would let Kingston fuck me up mentally.

Drying my tears, I cranked up my ride, put it into gear, and exited the hotel parking lot. Doing the dash, I flew home and made it there in to time. Storming into the house, I was relieved to see Memphis was gone. I didn't have time for his ass and he was liable to catch my wrath if he had been there. I was fed the fuck up and I needed to put my hands on something or someone. I was tired of muthafuckas taking my kindness for weakness, and the evil Tahleea was about to surface.

Running up to my bedroom, I headed straight for my closet. Grabbing my Louie luggage set, I opened them and sat them on the bed. Snatching any and everything I thought I might need, I threw it all into the suitcases. In the midst of me packing my shit, Dana began calling my phone. I let it continue to ring because I really didn't feel like talking to anyone. Besides, if I told her what I was about to do, she would only try to talk me out of it and try to make me come stay with her for a while. I didn't want that; I needed some time to myself to clear my head. I had way too much on my mind and it was only a matter of time before I ended up on Snapped. I definitely couldn't afford that. I was young and beautiful, with a very successful business that was only expanding by the day. I just had to remove myself from this toxic situation and regroup.

After filling my suitcase with all my necessities, I went into my secret safe behind a hidden wall I had in my closet. After punching in the combination, I opened it and took out the hundred grand I had stashed in it. Snatching one of my Gucci totes, I stuffed it all in and zipped it up. Putting my safe and wall back into place, I grabbed the tote full of cash and my suitcases and headed to my car. I had all my debit and credit cards, but Memphis had access to all my statements. I didn't want anyone to be able to find me, so I had the cash so I wouldn't leave a paper trail.

Unlocking my doors and popping my trunk, I hurriedly threw my suitcases in. I threw the tote full of money on the floor behind the driver's seat, the ran back into the house to grab my last suitcase. I was moving as quickly as possible because I didn't want Memphis to come home and catch me leaving. Snatching the last suitcase, I swiftly ran down the steps and out the door, locking it behind me. Throwing the luggage on the back seat, I closed the door and hopped into the driver's seat. After cranking up my car, I stopped for a second and sent Kingston a message.

You've hurt me to the core! I loved & trusted you with all of me and you promised that you would never break my heart, but that you did. I just hope it was all worth it, because you've lost the best thing that had ever happened to you. Take care Kingston Kennedy, just know I did love you. -Tahleea

I then dried the few tears that slipped from my eyes and made a phone call to Sprint customer care.

"Thank you for calling Sprint, this is Aaliyah; how may I assist you today?" the chirpy operator spoke through the phone.

"Hello, hi, I'm calling to change my number," I informed her. By the time Kingston would try to text or call back, my number wouldn't be the same.

I then placed my car into gear and headed for the freeway. I was headed for the airport. Where I would go; wherever there was a flight leaving tonight.

Chapter 13

Memphis

With my mind cleared, I was locked and loaded in the studio cooking up some new material. I must have lost track of time because when I opened the doors, the sun was rising over the trees.

Fuck, I thought to myself as I tried to cover my face from the sun's blinding rays. I pulled my phone out of my pocket and noticed that I hadn't missed much. Obviously, I wasn't a thought to my wife. She hadn't texted or called to see where I was. She was used to it. She knew that this career of mine required me to be away for long ass hours. Nonetheless, I needed to head home and shower before the day got started. I was expecting India to call or stop by at any moment. Instead of being surprised by her arrival, I decided to hit her up before she did me.

Good morning queen. I know that were supposed to link up this morning. Just hit me up and let me know when you're on your way. I'm about to shower so if you are on your way, hold off for about half an hour. -Memphis

Handle your business. I still haven't got up and got my day started. These pregnancy symptoms kicking my ass. –India

Typically, I would be upset bout that statement, but it gave me time to handle what I needed to and wash my ass. It also gave me time to get home and mend things over with the dragon I kept at the house. Even with all the intentions I had of leaving her stupid ass, a part of me wanted to smooth it over as best as I could. She just had to try not to piss me off in the process. I called her phone but got a weird ass message stating that the Sprint customer was unavailable. Knowing her, she probably forgot to pay her phone bill again and would expect me to do so once I got back home.

I pulled up expecting to see her car in the driveway, but it wasn't there. I walked into the house and there was a cold chill over it. I lifted the light switch and made my way into our bedroom. I walked in and noticed that shit was everywhere.

"This bitch man," I mumbled to myself. I ignored the mess on the bed and headed into our closet to grab me something to wear for the day.

"What the fuck?"

I pulled my phone out and immediately dialed her number. Again, I got the same message. Looking around at the empty hangers, I concluded that the bitch left me. She really fucking left. I walked out of the closet and began to search for answers as to why. I hadn't done anything out of my usual. Maybe I went overboard and she had finally had enough.

I went over to the bed and sat on it. I completely forgot about the mess she left, as I began to think about where she may have gone.

"She couldn't have went too far," I thought aloud as I called her shop.

"Cuteazz Couture. How may I help you?"

I knew the voice from a mile away.

"Dana, where is Tahleea?"

"Um, who is this and how can I help you?"

Her tone with from professional to ratchet in the blink of an eye.

"Man, don't play with me; you know damn well who this is. Put that bitch on the phone before I come down there and beat both y'all asses."

"TUH! Nigga, you ain't gone beat nobody's ass around here. You better calm that shit down. Besides, she ain't here. I been trying to call her ass all morning, but her phone is off."

"Yeah, aight. When she come in, tell her ass to call me. She got some shit she need to explain."

"WHATEVER!"

The phone call ended and I was still left with questions as to where she may have been. I sent India a text, in hopes that she may have spoken with her.

Aye, I know that this is a strange ass text, but have you talked to Tahleea lately? -Memphis

No, why? Have you talked to Kingston? Fuck kind of question is that? We cool but we don't talk like that. That's just messy. -India

India was right. I didn't know why I even sent the text to her, but it was a shot in the dark.

Oh ok, well if she hit you up, let me know. She got some shit to explain to me. -Memphis

India replied with a thumbs up but followed with another message.

You know that's funny that you did ask about her. The last time her and I interacted was on our spa date when I told her that I was pregnant. You should have saw the look on her face. It was almost one of jealousy. -India

A section of hell took over me. It hit me like a fucking ton of bricks. This bitch had opened her mouth and told my wife that she and I were expecting a kid. I couldn't believe how fucking stupid she was. I couldn't begin to put into words what I wanted to say, so I replied with a simple text message.

We gone talk about it when we link up. I'll be back at the studio in about an hour. Be there with the money so that I can handle this little transaction. -Memphis

She replied again with another thumbs up and it made me angry. Never in a million years would I think that she could be so got damn dumb. I stood to my feet and punched a hole into the wall. My wife was gone because my side bitch didn't know how to play her position, but she would soon learn how to.

I took my shower, got dressed, and headed back down to the studio. It was still early in the day, and I already needed a drink and a blunt. I tried throughout the morning to call Tahleea a few more times but continued to get the same result. I was growing angrier by the minute. Wherever she was, she had better stay there at this point. There was no telling what I was going to do to her.

Upon my arrival to the studio, I remembered how I could get in touch with her. I sent an email to her phone.

Hey, I don't know where you're at or what's going on but if you need me to get the phone cut back on, let me know. I was stuck in the studio all last night working, so I'm sorry about not making it to the house. Hit me up when you get this with the information to your sprint account and I'll get it handled for you.

Memphis

With that out the way, I felt a little less pressure in finding her. I knew that she would eventually open her email for something, whether it be for a client or just to check and make sure she hadn't missed any sales. My focus returned to my dumb ass side bitch in that instant. I walked over to the mini fridge I kept in the studio and pulled out a bottle. I rolled up a blunt and began to play some of the tracks that I'd spent most of the night working on. I took the entire blunt to the head in less than ten minutes, attempting to ease my mind before I was face to face with her. It wasn't working.

I began to work on another instrumental when I got a knock at my door. I took a deep breath and tried to gather my thoughts before I opened the door. I looked at the clock on the computer and she was late, but it wasn't unbearable.

I opened the door and, to my surprise, it wasn't who I anticipated. It was Hitman. I stood in the doorway looking around before I let him in.

"What's up my nigga?" he spoke as I looked around him.

"What's good, come on in."

I stepped to the side so that he could slide in next to me. He greeted me with a fist bump and the two of us fell back into the room. He got comfortable in one of the chairs and propped his feet up as he listened to the music playing.

"I like that shit. It's dope."

I nodded my head in agreeance. He then opened his mouth yet again.

"So, what's up man? You got that for me? I got to go drop that shit off."

I looked at him out the corner of my eye but kept my face turned towards the computer screen. "Nah. I don't yet."

He took a deep breath and his tone rose.

"Got damn man, come on. First, you tell me you can fuck with me on the whole thang, then drop it to half, tell me to meet you here; now, you telling me you ain't got the shit. Come on Memphis, man. This is my livelihood at stake."

I shrugged my shoulders. It wasn't my problem that he got into bed with the motherfuckers he did. I was being gracious by helping his ass out. I didn't owe him shit. All of this was off GP.

"I said nah, my nigga. I didn't say I wouldn't get it. I simply said nah, I ain't got it yet. It should be in route."

As I made the statement to him, I placed a text to India.

Yo, where you at? It's been over an hour. -Memphis

Hey, got caught up with something. I will call you when I'm on my way. Just stay at the studio. Will be there soon. Sorry about the delay. Miss you. -India

I sat in front of the computer screen reading over her text as I shook my head. "Fuck… just like a bitch. Can't be on time for shit," I mumbled to myself as I sent her a text back.

Aight man, just hurry up. I got other shit to do today and got people waiting on me. -Memphis

I turned towards Hitman and showed him the text. He shook his head as well but understood.

"Man, tell I-Key hurry the fuck up. This is a life or death situation."

"When it gets here, I will call you man; relax. Them folks done waited this long, they can wait another hour or so. I got you."

He shook his head and got up from his seat. I gave him another fist bump and turned back towards my computer screen, playing with different sounds. As he left, my phone began to ring. It was India.

"Hey, I'm about 15 minutes out. I got the run around at the bank, but I got the cash. I will see you in a second."

"Aight, hurry up. I got to talk to you about some shit when you get here."

"Ok, is everything ok?"

"It will be once we talk. Now, get yo ass here." I ended the call and placed my phone on the desk.

Twenty minutes later, there was another knock on the door. It was India. She walked in with a sundress on, some Dolce and Gabbana shades, and a pair of heels.

"Where the fuck you been?" I asked, looking her up and down.

"Damn, can I not get cute to come see you? I got to let you know that I ain't no basic bitch like that duck you got a home."

My demeanor changed and my fury grew. I tried to keep my face intact and at least get through our transaction. I just needed the money and to send her on her way. She placed the bag on the table and handed me the money. I looked at it for a moment, then sat it down.

"You ain't gone count it?"

"Should I have too?"

She shrugged her shoulders, then walked around me. She placed her hands on my shoulders and began to rub them. Noticing the bottle of alcohol on the table, she began to speak her peace on it.

"It's a little too early for you to be drinking, sir. You seem tense, is everything ok?"

Before I knew it, I had snapped on her. "Nah. I'm not ok. You and my wife been fucking pillow talking. Did you tell her you were pregnant by me?"

I grabbed her wrist and swung her body to the front of me. I stood to my feet and towered over her.

"Ok. You are tripping. Let me go because this shit hurts."

"Answer my question."

"Mario, let me the fuck go. She doesn't know who I'm pregnant by. Hell, I don't know who I'm pregnant by."

"That's bullshit!" I yelled and, before I knew it, my hand was across her face. Her body hit the floor and I stood like a raging bull, ready to strike once again.

She looked up at me as her eyes were slowly turning a purplish black tint. She began to cry slightly, and watching her on the ground submitting to me showed me that she was no different than the bitch I was married to.

"I guess you gone leave me like her ass did too now, huh? Take yo ass back home to that fucking square ass nigga. GET OUT!"

She picked herself up from the floor and maneuvered around me to get her belongings.

"Don't you touch that fucking money."

She didn't look in its direction. She made her way to the door but standing on the other side of it was Hitman. He looked at her, then stepped to the side so that she could get out of the room. He then looked at me as he walked in.

"I take it that we good now?"

I turned away and put my hand on my head, as reality set in on what I had just done. I motioned for him to give me a moment to gather my thoughts. He did, but he also noticed the stacks of money on the table. He pulled himself up a seat and I turned around.

"What the fuck you doing, man?"

"I'm just sitting here until you get yo shit together. I been in the parking lot waiting this whole time. I told you I need this shit asap."

I took a deep breath and counted 25k out of the 50. He looked at me with a side eye because he realized that there was much more money left over. He didn't say a word, but his demeanor spoke volumes.

"Aye man, I don't need this shit from you right now. Either you gone take it or leave it. That's half the boat, my nigga. Handle ya business."

He remained silent and took the money, stuffing it in various pockets. He got up from the table, staring me down the entire time as he reached the door. I walked over to it and closed it as he walked out. His car pulled out of the parking lot of my studio. I was left alone with 25K and my thoughts.

Chapter 14

Kingston

I felt some type of way about the text Tahleea sent me and I couldn't gather my thoughts in enough time to put it in a text. After the way shit transpired at the hotel, I felt out of my element. I tried to call her later that day several times but never got an answer. I gave it a rest and gave her the space she needed to ease her mind before I tried to reach out to her again. I couldn't keep her off my mind, which brought me to the realization that there was a damn snake in my house. Instead of going to my office, I decided to make a detour and head towards India's job.

I pulled up half an hour before noon and noticed that her car wasn't in sight. Walking into the building, I was greeted by a receptionist.

"Welcome, how can we assist you today?"

I looked at the name plate on the desk and gave her a warm smile. "I am here to see Mrs. Kennedy please. Can you get her and tell her that her husband is here?"

The woman coughed and cleared her throat. "Let me check and see if she is in. I was unaware that she was married. I've never noticed a ring on her hand."

I looked at the woman and brushed her statement off. I didn't think much of it. I'd known women in her line of work to separate their personal life from their business life for confidentiality reasons, so it wasn't that big of a deal.

"Uh sir, it doesn't look like Mrs. Kennedy is in today. She is actually off for the next few days. She hasn't been to work in a few days. Is there anything else that I can do for you?"

I placed my right hand on top of my head and the other on my waistline. India had taken vacation time and didn't tell me. That wasn't like her.

"No. You've done enough; thank you, sweetheart."

I turned to walk out of the building and, just as I did, my phone began to ring. It was India.

"Hey baby."

"What's up. Where are you?"

"What do you mean. I'm on my lunch break. Where are you?"

"I'm at your office. I was coming to see you so that we could talk over lunch, but I take it that's out the question."

"Oh well, yeah, sorry baby. I had to make a run. I guess the school didn't call you, but KJ is sick."

I didn't respond as I stood outside of her building looking around, hoping that she would just randomly pop up, surprising me. I waited for a couple more brief moments, but her breaking the silence let me know that I wasn't going to see her.

"Hello," she spoke through the speaker.

"Yeah, I'm still here and, no, they didn't but ok. Are you heading to the house when you're done?"

"I would think so, we have a sick child. Are you heading there?"

"If that's where you're going to be, then yes. Like I stated, we have to talk."

"What do we need to talk about Kingston?"

The deep breath she took let me know that I was aggravating her. She was becoming impatient with the conversation."

"It's not important at the moment. Get the boy home and settled, and I will see you when I get there."

She got quiet, as I heard her phone beep through the Bluetooth stereo system in her car. "Hey baby, let me call you back. I got another call coming in. I'll be headed towards the house soon, just meet me there and we can handle everything from that point."

The phone disconnected and I was stuck there once again, looking stupid at the expense of my wife. The shit was getting old and it was coming to an end sooner than she could realize. I just gave her those exact instructions and she completely heard none of it. Heading towards my car, I received an email alert to my phone.

50,000 dollars withdrawn from account 11:48 am. Thank you for banking with Wells Fargo. Have a great day.

I dialed India's number once more, but I was sent directly to the voicemail. I was unsure of the games that she was attempting to play, but she was about to play them alone. I got into my car and received a call from a private number.

"Watch yo bitch."

That was all that was said before the call disconnected. That was the third time in less than a week that I'd heard those words and it was time to find out why but, before I did that, I had to try once more to find Tahleea. I was starting to get concerned about her.

I placed a call to her shop to see if she had gone there.

“Hello, thank you for calling Cuteazz Couture. How may I help you?

“Yes, is the owner of the business in?”

“She’s not. Is there anything that I can do for you.”

“Yes, will you tell her that King called for her. She will know who I am.”

“King, as in Kingston. Hey man, this is Dana. I don’t know where she is. She’s had clients calling and emailing her all day. I’m getting a little overwhelmed but, if I speak to her, I will let her know that you are trying to find her as well.”

“Thank you, Dana. Have a great day.”

As the call ended, I got into my car and placed my head on the steering wheel. I could only hope that she was safe wherever she was. I didn’t like not knowing where she was. Not talking to her made a part of me feel empty, especially how the way we parted. Exhaling, I began to drive. I decided to stop at CVS on the way home and it may have been a good thing. I received a call from Hitman.

“Hello.”

“Kingston. We need to talk. Meet me at your office as soon as possible.”

“Give me a couple hours. I have a situation I need to handle at home first, then I’ll be there.”

I didn’t have the slightest clue as to what he wanted, but one thing was for sure; him reaching out to me had nothing but bad news surrounding it. It was just one more thing added to the list of shit already on my overflowing plate.

Chapter 15

India

"Fuck!" I screamed as I threw my phone into the cup holder and began bearing my fist into the palm of my hand. I was beginning to drown in lies and, yet, I had just told my husband a few more. I had to find an excuse for me not being at my office, and our son being sick was the first thing that came to mind at that moment. Still sitting in the parking lot of Memphis' studio, I began to break out into sobs. My life, that was once happy as hell, was starting to crumble right before my eyes, all because I couldn't control my temptation. I couldn't blame anyone but myself though. Grabbing some tissues from my purse, I began to pat the blood that was stained on my bottom lip. I couldn't believe that Memphis laid his hands on me because he thought I'd ran my mouth off to his wife. She knew I was pregnant because I told her, but that was before I even knew who the father really was. I didn't understand why he didn't believe me but, if he laid hands on her the way he had done me, it's clear as to why she had left his ass. Out of all the years we'd been together, Kingston had never laid a finger on me unless he was pleasing my body; and here I was betraying him by messing around with this woman abuser. Pulling myself together, I dried my eyes and started my car. Pulling out of the studio parking lot, I made my way to the mall to grab some makeup from MAC. Once I got it, I quickly beat my face and hurriedly drove to KJ's school. When I got there, my baby and his fellow classmates were engaging in finger painting. He looked so happy and he had paint all over his little cheeks.

"Hi Mrs. Kennedy, are you here to take my little buddy KJ away from us early today?" one of the teachers asked as she approached me.

"Unfortunately, yes, I'm sorry. I know I should've called, but I've been so busy today; it slipped my mind," I told her, giving her a slight smirk. The teachers at the school just loved my son to pieces. They hated to see me pick him up, especially early.

"Aw man! Well, I wish you would've remembered to call. I would've had him all cleaned up and ready. But I can clean him up real fast, it's no biggie," she stated. "Go ahead and sign him out Mrs. Kennedy; I'll have him ready in no time," she continued as she walked off towards KJ. I watched as she picked him up and carried him to the bathroom as they talked. I assumed she was explaining to him that I was there to pick him up. After they were out of my sight, I picked up the pen and clipboard and commenced to signing him out. When I was finished, I walked over to his cubby and grabbed his belongings.

"Mommyyyy!!!" KJ squealed with the look of bliss upon his face as he ran at me full speed.

"Hey, my baby!" I replied while scooping him up into my arms, giving him the biggest hug.

"Mommy, you look so pretty!" He smiled while rubbing my cheek, referring to the makeup I had on.

"Awww, thank you mommy's baby!" I said, kissing his cheek and softly pinching his nose. I swear, the little guy gave me life. Just looking into his innocent eyes made me forget about all the shit that I was going through. Putting him down next to me, I grabbed his hand.

"Tell your teachers and friends bye lil man, so that we can go," I told him. KJ did as he was asked and said his goodbyes, and the two of us walked out of his school hand in hand. When we made it to the car, I put KJ in the back seat and strapped the safety belt around him. I then closed him in, walked around the car, and got into the driver's seat.

After buckling up, I cranked the engine and headed into the direction of our home. In less than twenty minutes, we were pulling into our driveway and Kingston had beat me there. My heart began to pound frivolously because KJ was far from sick and I didn't know how I would pull of the lie. As I thought quickly, I immediately turned my attention to my son.

"Hey lil man, you wanna play a game with mommy?" I asked.

"Yes!" he replied with big excited grin plastered across his face, as he shook his head up and down.

"Okay, great! We're going to play the doctor game. I'm the nurse, you're the patient, and daddy's the doctor."

"Daddy? But daddy's not here mommy," he interrupted me.

"Yes, he is; daddy's in the house and he wants to play too. So, you have to play a good patient and act like you're sick so that me and daddy can take care of you. Can you do that for mommy?" I asked, hoping and praying that he wouldn't mess this up for me.

"Yes, mommy, I can do that!" he said. He then began to cough and planted a sad expression in his face. "See mommy, I'm sick!" he said.

"Good job baby. Now, you have to keep acting like this when we get inside the house with daddy, okay? He has to believe that you're sick or the game won't work, okay!?" I informed him.

"Okay mommy!" he agreed, nodding his little head. Grabbing my purse, I hopped out of the car and walked around to get him out. Opening his door, I reached in, picked him up, and laid his head onto my shoulder. Closing the door, I took a deep breath and headed towards the door.

"Ready Mommy? We're gonna get daddy good!" KJ whispered with a slight snicker. Deep down, I felt bad as fuck for bringing my son into my web of lies, but there was no turning back now. When I approached the door and placed the key inside of the hole, the door flew open and Kingston was standing behind it.

"Heeey little buddy!" He immediately grabbed KJ from my arms. "Mommy told me you weren't feeling too well. What's the matter man?" he asked while holding him tight, rubbing his back. KJ began to cough.

"I don't feel good daddy; my head and stomach hurts," he stated weakly. My baby was acting his role to a tea, and I couldn't be more relieved.

"Here, let me take him upstairs and lay him down," I said, grabbing him back and heading upstairs. Kingston gave me the side eye.

"Yea, okay! And meet me in the bedroom when you finish because we need to talk!" he said sternly. I just nodded my head yes as I continued up to our son's room. When I made it there, I slightly closed the door.

"But, mommy, I don't wanna go to bed; I'm not sleepy!" KJ whined as I stripped him from his clothing.

"Shhh, keep your voice down baby. Listen, you don't have to go to sleep; this is just part of the game. I just need you to lay here for a while under the covers. I'll cut on the cartoons and you can watch tv, okay!" I whispered as I got him dressed into some pjs.

"Okaaay," he said with a pouting lip. I instantly began to feel bad for making him play along in my mess.

"Aw baby! I promise when the game is over, mommy will take you out for ice cream and any toy you want." I began to bribe him and his eyes instantly lit up.

"Okay mommy, I'll lay down, but can I watch Avengers cartoons?" he asked.

"Yes, baby, you can watch anything you like," I replied. I then tucked him in, grabbed the remote, and turned on what he requested. "Okay baby, mommy is going to go talk to daddy. Call me if you need me, okay," I told him.

"Okay!" he replied with his eyes glued to the tv. I then kissed his forehead and made my way to our bedroom to see what Kingston needed to talk about. I really didn't want to hear it because deep down, I already knew what it was, but I was going to have to face the music sooner or later. When I walked into the room, Kingston had his phone in his hand and he was pacing back and forth across the floor.

"What's up with you?" I asked, turning up my lip. I must've startled him because he jumped at the sound of my voice.

"Aw, nothing. But here, go piss on this real quick," he said, grabbing a EPT pregnancy test off the dresser and handing it to me. I instantly cut my eyes at him and stormed off to the bathroom. When I turned to close the door, he was right on my heels with his foot in the door.

"Jeezus Kingston, really? What the hell or you doing?" I asked, frustrated.

"I coming in, I wanna see." He looked me up and down. Taking a deep frustrated breath, I stepped to the side and let him in.

"Damn, so now you don't trust that I'll piss on the stick?" I barked.

"Nah, it ain't that. I just wanna be right here with you every step of the way, just like I was with KJ," he said while leaning against the sink, making himself comfortable. I then rolled my eyes and walked over to the toilet. Pulling up my dress and pulling down my panties, I squatted down and peed onto the tip of the test. When I was finished, I placed the cap on the tip, wiped my lady parts, and flushed the toilet. Pulling up my panties, I fixed my clothing and glimpsed at the test. It was only one line, so I hurried up and showed him before the second one appeared.

"See, I'm not pregnant!" I quickly flashed it in his face then tried to turn and trash it, but he quickly snatched it from my grasp. He then looked at it and began shaking his head.

"Why do you feel the need to keep lying to me, India? This test clearly says positive!" he seethed, showing me the double lines. He then threw it onto the ground towards my feet. "You care to explain why the hell you've been constantly denying the fact that your carrying a whole fucking child of mine!" he screamed, and I could see the veins popping from his neck. It had been a while since I had seen him this upset. My heart began to pound uncontrollably as I tried to think of my next lie. "Why you so damn quiet now? Cat got ya tongue?" he continued. I stood there frozen in my thoughts, as I continued to think of a good explanation. Kingston let out a slight chuckle. "Aight! Well, let me ask you something else you may can tell me the answer to." He clenched his jaws tightly as he walked closer to me.

"Why did I get this text earlier alerting me that you withdrew fifty grand from one of our accounts today?" he asked, showing me the message alert from Wells Fargo. I cursed myself on the inside because I thought I was extra careful and withdrew from the account that wasn't connected to his message alerts. Apparently, my dumb ass screwed up yet again.

"I… I told you that I was lending money to Tahleea, honey. I got the money this morning and took it to her," I lied, reaching out for him to caress his chest. Kingston immediately backed away so that I wouldn't touch him.

"Arrrggghhh!" he screamed as he turned and punched the wall. "Dammit, India! So, you're just going to keep fuckin lying to me, huh? Like I'm just some big ass fool!" he seethed.

"What?! Kingston, I'm not lying to you!"

"Yea, you are! You lying dead to my fuckin face and you know for a fact you are! It makes me question what the hell else you've been fuckin lying about!" he continued.

"Kingston, you sound crazy! I haven't lied to you about anything and keep your voice down; our son is sick!" I snapped. Kingston scoffed as he paced back and forth across the bathroom floor.

"Yea, right! I wouldn't be surprised if you lied about that!" He called me out.

"What!? Do you really think I would lie about our son being ill?" I asked, and he immediately scoffed again.

"To tell the truth, India, I don't know what you'd do anymore." He shook his head. I sucked my teeth and cut my eyes at him. As soon as I was about to defend myself, KJ came running into our room full speed.

"Mommy, Mommy! I don't wanna play doctor anymore. I wanna go get my ice cream and toy now!"

Chapter 16

Kingston

I stood in the doorway dumbfounded, as I listened to my son rat his mother out. I looked at my wife with an even dumber look. This motherfucker really had me fucked up.

"Really, India. You even got my fucking son lying to me?"

I turned my attention to KJ and picked him up from the ground. I took my hand and placed it against his forehead. He felt perfectly fine. I couldn't believe the shit that was going on under the roof of my own home. I released KJ from my arms.

"Hey, big man, if you want ice cream, you'll get some later. Right now, I need you to go back to your room and watch tv. Me and mommy need to finish talking."

"Can I have my toy too?"

"You can have the world son. If that's what you want, you can have two of them. Sound good?" I placed my fist out, awaiting him to bump it with his. He did and, with a big smile on his face, he skipped happily towards his room. I looked back at India with fury in my eyes. My rage burned deep in my soul.

"India, what the fuck is your problem?"

She hung her head in shame and refused to look up at me.

"Answer me!" I demanded, speaking through my teeth. "You acting brand fucking new lately. Your hair is different, your choice in clothing is different, your fucking movement is different. Hell, since when did you start wearing anything more than lipstick and eye liner? What the fuck is this shit?"

I reached out and smeared the foundation from her cheek, noticing that there was a black mark under her eye. "What the fuck happened to you, India?"

She looked up at me and shook her head, nothing. I shook my fucking head at the ground and took a deep breath.

"If I wasn't a smarter man, I would think that you fucking around on me, but I know better India. You're a boss in your own right, but you wouldn't jeopardize everything we've built together. With that being said, I'm going to give you one more chance to be honest with me."

She didn't say a word. She remained silent on the bed. I clenched my fist and pulled both my hands towards my mouth. I blew a massive amount of air out, trying to calm myself down.

"You don't want to talk, fuck it. I'm done trying. This shit is getting old. You've lie about the pregnancy, you've lied about KJ, you've lied about the money, which you're about to get up and go get."

The more I began to think of the shit she lied about, my rage began to escalate once again.

"Damn India, so that's what we come down to? I can't believe that, after all the years, you would shut me out like this. You still don't have shit to say for yourself? No? Don't worry about it though. If this is the way our marriage is going to go, then it is what it is. I'll be back to get my shit and we'll settle shit in court about KJ. I'm done."

I took my wedding band off and tossed in to her. I walked out of the room and headed towards the front door.

"KJ!" I barked out.

He came sprinting towards me with a towel wrapped around his neck. "I'm not KJ… I'm Super Junior. How can I help you, sir?"

He managed to put a smile on my face through all the bullshit. I picked him up and touched his chest. "Daddy needs to use some of these super powers man. I'll bring them back when I come back for you. In the meantime, I need you to be a big boy for me. Daddy will be gone for a little while. Do you think that you can hold down the secret hideout for me until I return?"

"But I thought we were getting ice cream."

I played along with him as his face dropped. "KJ, is that you? I thought Super Junior was here."

"I don't want to play super heroes anymore, daddy. I want to go with you and get ice cream."

I held him tighter and took a deep breath. "Listen buddy, right now, daddy has to go take care of some business. I promise that we will go to Ice Cream Mountain and I will let you eat as much as that little stomach can handle. You just have to let me handle this situation first. Can you do that for me?"

He stuck his pinky out and waited for me to lock mine. "Pinky promise," he uttered.

"Pinky promise." I placed him on the ground and looked up at India, as she stood at the end of the foyer.

"Listen to your mother while I'm gone. Even if what she tells you something she shouldn't."

I looked up at her with disgust and turned to walk out of the house. Just as I got into my car, I looked at my text messages. It was Hitman.

I'm at yo office. Get here asap. -Hitman

I took a deep breath and prepared my head to deal with the nutcase waiting for me. I didn't know what he wanted to talk about, but I was sure it had something to do with the money that he previously asked for.

Half an hour passed before Hitman and I were face to face. The room was filled with tension. His nostrils we flared as he eyed me the entire time I walked towards my seat. There was an obvious issue that needed to be addressed in the room.

"So, what's up? What can I do for you, Hitman?"

He sat back in his seat and ran his tongue over his gold slugs. "Kingston, I need that money man. Fuck that percentage. I need that paper man."

I shook my head. "It don't work like that man. The deal is done. Once the paperwork was finalized, there's noting that I can do."

"Nah, my nigga, that ain't how this works. If it's a will, it's a way. I need you to make that shit happen big dawg. I got a bigger situation that could potentially take me away from the fam. I can't have that happening right now. I got too much on the line. I need you to reverse that shit. Get on the phone, call them other rich motherfuckers, and make the shit happen."

I shook my head no once more. "Maybe you misunderstood the statement I just made. There isn't shit I can do about it right now. Even if I called, they are going to tell you the same shit I'm telling you. Trust me, man; you got a much better situation with the deal done. You'll constantly have income coming in."

"Fuck that man."

He stood to his feet and began pacing back and forth around the room. "FUCK!" he yelled at the top of his lungs.

"Yo man, I'm gone need you to calm that shit down. This is still a place of business."

"Fuck yo business, Kingston."

He slammed both his fist into my desk and rattled my belongings. I stood to my feet and loosened my tie. With all the bullshit that I was facing, he was on the verge of bringing an old version of me out.

"What's the problem, my nigga?" I questioned, rolling the sleeves of my shirt up.

He smirked as he looked on at me adjusting myself. "Niggas like you is my problem, man. You niggas get the world handed to you and forget where the fuck you come from."

I smirked as I unhooked my watch from my wrist. "Nigga, I ain't forgot shit. I just learn to evolved with the shit that was moving around me. Now, either we talk like grown ass men or we settle this shit like we would have in the hood."

"Kingston, you don't want these problems nigga. Sit yo ass down. I'm here on business. I don't fight no more. You forget I evolved into a killer. Don't be a victim."

His idle threats held no weight. He eased his nerves long enough for him to sit down. I did the same and we both calmed ourselves down.

"So, what's the real issue Hitman?"

He took a deep breath and clenched his fist in the palm of his hand. "You know the woman you had working for you prior to that young girl you got in there?"

I pondered for a second before I answered. "Tonya? Yes, what about her?"

"Yeah, that's my wife. To make a long story short, man this bitch done had a baby on me and she thinks that I don't know it's not mine. She's always wanted a child, but I couldn't give her one. We always talked about adopting but could never find an agency to give us a chance, considering my criminal background. I had a feeling that it would eventually be a problem in our relationship and, about a year ago, she started to act differently. I started to notice the change in the way she was coming home. She was usually full of life and energetic. She slowly started to change as her hours grew. I had a suspicion that she may have started to fuck around with someone else, but never in a million years did I expect her to get pregnant, but you knew about that. You were around her the whole time she was here. Which brings me to my next question. Did you ever see her with another nigga?"

I shook my head no, as he continued.

"When she told me, I played it off like I was the happiest man in the world but, deep down, I'm fucking broken behind it. It kills me that I can't give my wife a child due to me being fixed, but that was a decision I decided to make after my baby mama became a bitch from hell. I told myself that I would never do it again; now, I'm regretting it. That bitch means the world to me, so I'll never show her how bad she truly hurt me but, once I know for sure who the nigga is that did it, I'm taking his life into my hands. That one thing is a fact.

The one thing about her is that she wears her ring faithfully, so there is no excuse as to why he decided to disrespect my situation. On top of everything else, she told me that you ain't gone let her come back to work. I'm just trying to figure out why. I know she worked hard. Hell, she was here every day. Most times on overtime, so what the fuck is the issue? This shit has got me in a bigger bind than I need to be."

I took a deep breath and swallowed my spit. My nerves got bad immediately, as I processed the information.

"OK… ok… wait, let's rewind to the beginning. Tonya is your wife?"

He shook his head yes.

I sat back in my seat and propped my feet up on my desk, twirling a pen. I couldn't believe the shit that I was hearing. Furthermore, I didn't understand why she would tell him that I wouldn't give her the job back. As I recall, she gave me her resignation verbally, but I couldn't risk blowing everything that was beneath the surface now.

"Look man, first things first, I'm sorry about your wife getting pregnant. If I could search the office to find out who she may have been spending time with, I would but, honestly, I don't have the time to investigate every one of my employees." I swallowed a massive amount of my saliva and finished thinking through the statement to come. "As far as her job, things are just tight around here at the moment and I filled her position, anticipating her wanting to stay home with the baby. I never knew her husband, i.e. you were the nigga she always talked about. She always explained how you were always on the go grinding so that she wouldn't have to work so hard."

"Yeah, man. I try my hardest to make sure that she doesn't have to exert herself. She was happy here, man. This was the one thing that she had going for her. I just don't get it man. I know you can create a job and bring her back in."

I looked at my computer screen and pretended to pull some reports up. I didn't want him to realize that I was bullshitting my way through our conversation.

"Right now, man, it ain't shit that I can do. I'm overstaffed as it is and the last thing I'm going to do is let someone go right now. It's the middle of my peak season. As much as I miss her working for me, I can't take that chance right now."

He placed his head in his palms and I heard his breathing pattern change. "Fuck!"

There was obviously more to this situation that I was missing. Hitman was a hustler; he had ways to get money, so it wasn't like he was pressed for it.

"Kingston, look man, I need her to have this job. If not, I need that money. You not understanding. I don't want to do what I have to do to get it, but you leaving me no choice."

I looked at him confused, attempting to gain an understanding. His tone and demeanor didn't sit well with me.

"At this point, that 50k mean more than the niggas I owe. That was her salary for the year. I'm gone need you to come off that Kingston You don't understand the shit we going through. This shit is life or death."

"Listen, I understand your concern with the situation but, even if I brought her back today, she wouldn't get that 50k up front. I don't know what kind of game y'all trying to run here, but it ain't gone fly. I suggest you use the resources that both you and I know that you have to get the money. There ain't shit that I can do right now. Just like you got shit going on at home, so do I."

Shrugging my shoulder like MJ after his sixth three, I had spoken my peace. Of course, I knew that it wouldn't sit well with him, but I was firm in my place and statement. I was done speaking on the situation.

Hitman just sat with his nostrils still flared, rocking back and forth while looking at me. He got up from his seat and moved towards the door. "Say no more my nigga. I hope your wife ready to kiss her husband goodbye. I'll see you soon Kingston."

He exited my office and I placed both of my fists on the desk. How did I never notice that her husband was Hitman? Furthermore, why did she get me caught up in this bullshit with her? My life was spiraling quickly and I had to find a way to grasp its reins again. My mind was in a thousand places at once as I sat back in my seat, looking at the ceiling. I needed to talk to the one person that knew me but was still missing in action.

I took a deep breath and began to open my desk drawers back and forth on some bored shit; then, it hit me as I watched Mario's phone sliding back and forth. I pulled it out and hit the power button. To my surprise, it came on. I hoped that he didn't have a lock on it or that he at least hadn't had it disconnected yet. If I could at least see a message from her on his screen, I would have felt better.

The apple logo began to spin, as the phone ran through its opening menu. Of course, it was locked, but there were messages popping up like crazy on the front of the screen. I noticed that most were from Tahleea trying to contact him, but most of the messages were old. Then, the slew of random women texting him, solidifying everything she'd told me about him.

There was one woman in particular that was blatantly disrespectful, but it was quite entertaining. As I began to scroll up and down the lock screen and read some of the shit she'd sent him, I couldn't help but to shake my head. If he was a bachelor, I would be rather jealous of his lifestyle. He had this woman lying in the bed with her husband, texting him the shit that she wanted to do to him. Her name was saved as Ikea in the phone. I could only hope that her husband never found the messages and, if he did, she was probably already dead.

I powered his phone back down and picked mine up. I placed a call to Tahleea, hoping that she would answer.

"The sprint number that you've dialed has been changed, disconnected, or is no longer in service."

What the fuck? I thought to myself. With fifty thousand dollars, you would think she would have paid her bill. I tried to call her office once more, but it went to the voicemail.

Chapter 17

Memphis

A full week passed and that motherfucking bitch of mine had yet to make an attempt to call me or come home. I was going crazy. It wasn't that I was in my feelings or no shit like that but, even with the shit that I'd taken her through, she'd never not come home. She had better have a damn good reason as to why she wasn't around. Putting all the negative thoughts and energy to rest, I decided that it was time for me to go find the answers myself.

"Damn, I must have really fucked up this time," I thought aloud to myself as I rode down the highway. Before making it to her office, I stopped at a florist. I grabbed the biggest bouquet of assorted flowers that I could find. I guess, in so many ways, that shit was eating at me, not having her at home. As I pulled up at her office, I noticed that her car wasn't there. I took a deep breath and got out of my car.

"Welcome to Cuteazz..."

Dana froze in midsentence when she picked her head up from beneath the front counter, noticing me.

"What's up?" I asked while looking around the shop, trying to see if I could spot Tahleea.

"She ain't here Memphis. I got a client. You'll have to come back later," Dana spat as she rolled her eyes in my direction.

I noticed movement in the back room. It almost looked like someone was hiding. I placed the flowers down on the counter and began to walk into the back.

"She ain't here. Yeah… aight…"

Making my way into the back, I noticed that it was relatively a mess.

"Tahleea… Tahleea… you got until I get to three to get out here. Don't make me have to come find yo ass."

There was a dead silence in the room, as Dana came rushing towards me. She grabbed my arm and tried to pull me out of the room.

"Memphis, I just told you she ain't here."

"One…"

"Memphis, you are tripping. Please don't make me call the police."

"Two…"

Dana was scratching at my arm, trying to get me to leave. Just as I was about to turn to knock her ass down, I heard a cough whose sound was familiar.

"Got yo ass… three."

I opened the door to the dressing room and, to my displeasure, it was a woman trying on a new dress. The woman was half naked, but her body was bad. She let out a loud scream and covered herself, pushing the door closed.

"Memphis, what the fuck? You scaring my client. I just told yo stupid ass that she wasn't here. I haven't seen her. She ain't been around here in over a week. Can you just leave?"

I began to migrate away from the room, back towards the showroom. "So, you ain't seen her ass either? Has she tried to call you, text, anything? I just need to make sure the bitch is alive at this point."

"No, Memphis, but maybe if you called her by her name instead of bitch, you would know something by now."

I balled my fist up and shrugged my shoulders in Dana's direction. She flinched swiftly.

"Fuck I thought, scary bitch. If that motherfucker bring her ass around here, tell her I was looking for her." I looked at the flowers I'd just bought and I slapped them off the counter. "Tell her she got 24 hours to contact me or else she need not never return."

I headed out the door to my car. My suspicions grew as to where she was because no matter what, Tahleea was about her business. She was always running her own shop but, now that I knew she wasn't there, something was definitely wrong. I put my bullshit aside and began to clear my head to think like a real nigga should when his bitch was missing in action.

Chapter 18

Tahleea

“Thank you, can I please have two lemons as well?” I asked the waiter as he sat my glass of sweet tea down onto the table.

“Sure ma’am, I’ll be right back with those,” he told me as he switched off. It was clear, by the way he popped his hips when he walked, that he had a little sugar in his tank. I giggled on the inside because he was trying so hard. I was at Planet Hollywood, overlooking the Vegas Strip while treating myself to a delicious lunch. I had been in Vegas for about a week, living it up like I had no care in the world; but no matter how much I gambled, shopped and partied, I still couldn’t help but to think about everything I had going on back home. I had even hit fifty grand on the Russian Roulette table, and I was still down. I missed Kingston so much, but my pride just would not let me call him. I was still fucked up behind the whole baby thing and I really didn’t want to hear any of his excuses. I was tired of excuses at this point. I did feel bad for just leaving Dana though. She had no clue as to where I was, and I knew she was probably worried sick about me. I had received a million emails from clients and another million from Memphis’ sorry ass. At first, they were sweet but, after I replied that I was alive after the first few, he began to curse me out and talk crazy.

Taking a deep breath, I pulled out my phone and called Dana. I called her cell twice and, both times, it went straight to voice mail. Looking down at my baby-faced Rolex, I figured she would probably be at the shop, so I called there. Just as I thought, she was there.

“Cuteazz Couture, this is Dana; how may I help you?” she answered.

“Hey boo, what are you doing?” I asked her.

"BOSS LADY!" she screamed into my ear, almost bursting my ear drum.

"Yea, it's me," I replied, feeling bad as hell.

"I HAVE BEEN WORRIED CRAZY ABOUT YO ASS! WHERE THE FUCK ARE YOU? MEMPHIS HAS BEEN LOOKING FOR YOU, COMING UP IN THE DAMN SHOP ACTING LIKE A FUCKIN MAD MAN, SCARING CLIENTS AND SHIT! KINGSTON CALLS DAMN NEAR EVERY DAY TO SEE IF I'VE HEARD FROM YOU. I'VE SENT YOU EMAILS AND EVERYTHING! WHY WOULD YOU CHANGE YOUR NUMBER? I'VE BEEN IN THIS MUTHAFUCKA BY MYSELF FOR THE PAST WEEK SLAVING, TRYING TO GET THESE ORDERS OUT AND KEEP THIS COMPANY AFLOAT! AND HERE YOU ARE CALLING LIKE EVERYTHING IS LILLIES AND ROSES! HOW DARE YOU, BOSS LADY! YOU BETTER TELL ME SOMETHING!" She yelled at me, barely taking a breath. I couldn't blame her for being so irate, so I took a deep breath before beginning to explain myself.

"I know, I know, I'm sorry," I said sincerely. "But hear me out, please?" I asked of her.

"Mmhm, I'm listening!" she replied dryly with a little attitude.

"I've been stressed out and overwhelmed with the shit going on at home with me and Memphis. I just got tired and fed up; I had to leave Dana," I said, not mentioning the shit going on with me and Kingston I was too embarrassed to share that part with her. As far as she knew, me and Kingston were picture perfect and it was going to remain that way. Dana sat silent on the other end of the phone.

"Hello," I stated, making sure she was still there.

"Yea, I'm here," she said, all stank.

"Well, why aren't you saying anything?"

"Because you asked me to hear you out, but I can't honestly take you serious right now. If you were going to tell me a lie, why did you call?"

"Huh? What do you mean?" I asked her.

"Look boss lady, I know you like the back of my hand. Every day you go through the same bullshit with Memphis and you've never pulled no bullshit like this. Your company and Kingston has always been your outlet. If you've ever needed to talk or vent, you've always called on me. I'm far from stupid, so when you're ready to be honest and tell me what's really going on, then you call me back," she seethed.

Rolling my eyes to the top of my head, I exhaled. I didn't know how Dana knew me so well, but you would think I came out of her twat instead of my mother's, the way she read me so good.

"Okay, Dana, damn! I ran away because me and Kingston are on bad terms," I confessed.

"Okay and what could be so bad that you run away and leave your company and best friend without warning? Is it that bad that the two of you couldn't talk it out, kiss and make up?" she shot back and I grew silent. "Uhhm, hello!" she sang.

"It's not that simple Dana. He violated in the worst way, I'm so hurt!" I began to break out in tears. Dana's tone immediately changed.

"Oh, hell nah, what that muthafucka do!?" she asked filled with rage. I tried catching my breath through sobs, so that I could began to explain.

"He had a baby on me, Dana!"

"With his wife? But, you knew that already. I was with you when she told you at the spa that she was pregnant," she said in confusion.

"No, nooo, no! He had a baby by the secretary at his company; the baby is already born Dana!" I said, breaking down once more.

"Oooh noooo! Are you sure? Did you ask him about it?" she questioned.

"He told me himself," I said through sniffles.

"Oh no, oh gawd no! I can't believe what I'm hearing. How could he do this to you?" she said sympathetically.

"Tuh, that's the same thing I said. I trusted him Dana. He led me to believe that I was the only one, that he was so in love with me. How could I be so stupid?!" I stated, still bawling like a big baby.

"I just can't believe Kingston! And that was my boy, he is so perfect for you. Have you talked to him? Did he say how it happened? Maybe there's a good explanation for this. I just can't see him having a baby on you out of spite, boss lady. Kingston don't move like that, at least I thought he didn't," she stated on his behalf.

"That's the thing. I didn't hear him out. I was so angry and hurt that I just walked out on him. Then, I went home, packed my bags, changed my number, and headed to the airport. I miss him so much Dana, but my stubbornness just won't let me call him," I told her.

"Well, he's been calling here looking for your ass like crazy, so I know he misses you too. Just call him boss lady and hear him out. You can't just shut him out like that. Kingston's a good dude, and I know you still love him."

"Like crazy," I shot.

"Well, there you go. Girl, you better call him up and come home and get that man back," she warned me.

"You right. I'ma call him," I assured her.

"Where yo ass at anyway?" she asked boldly.

"I'm in Vegas."

"VEGAS?!" she screamed. "You mean to tell me you in Vegas living it up and parlaying without me, while I'm here running yo damn company like a chicken with my head cut off?! Aw bitch, you owe me big time," she continued.

"Oh, hush, Dana," I said with a slight giggle. I knew she was going to fly off the hinges when I told her where I was. "I didn't plan on coming here. I just went to the airport and told them to give me their next flight out. I didn't care where it was going," I told her.

"Yea, yea, you just call Kingston and handle your business, so you can bring your ass back to Seattle and run this damn shop!" she spat.

"Uggh, I am. I'm about to call him now. Most likely I'll be back tomorrow or the day after, depending on if I can get a flight."

"Okay boo, just make sure you call and keep me posted," she replied.

"I promise, I will."

"Okay babe. Love you."

"I love you too, boo!" I shot back before ending the call. I then immediately scrolled through my contacts and called up my Zaddy, Kingston. After the first two rings, I was sent to voicemail. Taking a deep breath, I called back and got the same thing. Getting irritated, I decided to give it a rest and try back later. Holding my hand up to grab the waiter's attention, he came over and I asked him for my tab. Once he returned with it, I paid it, tipped him a hefty tip, and commenced to get up and leave. As I stood up from the table, I felt a sharp, excruciating pain shoot through my abdomen, causing me to hurdle over and scream out in pain.

"Oh no, Mrs. Carter, are you okay?" the waiter asked, running to my aid. The pain shot through again, becoming unbearable, and I dropped to my knees in tears. I didn't know what matter was, but I had never felt so much pain in my life.

"Do I need to get you medical attention honey?" The waiter asked while holding on to my arm, trying to stand me to my feet, but it was to no avail. The pain was beginning to shoot through my legs and I began to break out into a drenching sweat. The waiter's voice was beginning to become faint, and everything began to spin.

"Someone call me an ambulance please!" I could hear the waiter say before I passed out.

✳✳✳✳

I awoke in Sunrise Hospital in one of their hospital beds, with the bright ass hospital lights hurting my eyes. I was hooked up to a heart monitor, and I had an IV in my arm, pumping fluids into my body. I looked around the room and there was not one nurse or doctor in sight. Reaching over onto the side of my bed, I pressed the nurse call button.

"Do you need your nurse?" someone spoke through the monitor.

"Yes, please," I replied.

"Okay, let me find her and I'll send her right in."

"Thank you," I shot back. A few minutes passed and a brunette head, Caucasian lady came walking into my room.

"Hey Mrs. Carter, you're finally awake. Are you feeling okay?" she asked.

"Yes, I mean, I guess. What happened to me?" I asked, confused and scared at the same time.

"Well, you passed out at the restaurant and the ambulance brought you here. You're fine though; you were just dehydrated and your stress levels were very high. But don't worry, you and the little one are going to be okay. Just rest up a little bit more and we will discharge you," she told me, throwing me for a loop.

"Wait, what? Little one? What are you talking about?" I asked with the screw face.

"Your baby! Wait, you didn't know you were expecting?"

"Uhm no, you have to be mistaken," I assured her.

"No ma'am, I'm very sure that you're pregnant Mrs. Carter," she said, reaching over onto the counter and handing me a sonogram photo. My mouth immediately dropped, as I seen the little fetus on it with my name printed across the top. "We had to do an ultrasound to make sure everything was alright, due to you passing out," she informed me. Tears began to stream down my cheeks as I stared at the picture. Out of all my pregnancies, I had never made it far enough to get an ultrasound.

“Is the baby going to make it?” I asked.

“Yes ma’am! Why would you ask such a thing?” she stated, confused.

“Uhm, no reason. Can I just have a second please?” I asked her.

“Sure, just press the button again if you need me,” she stressed before leaving me alone. I sat there in deep thought for a moment. I was in total disbelief that I had a healthy fetus inside of me. Reaching for my phone, I dialed Kingston’s number once more. I needed to speak with him, and I needed to speak with him fast.

Chapter 19

Kingston

"Thank you for coming. I truly appreciate your business," I spoke as I stood to my feet, to shake yet another satisfied customer hand.

Work had been a steady flow of busy lately. I honestly hadn't put as much effort into my business as I had in the past week, ever. It was a good thing as well. I had still not heard from Tahleea. There were so many thoughts running through my mind as to where she was, but I couldn't allow myself to go into the dark about it. I knew that she was safe wherever she was. It would only be a matter of time before she returned to me.

As I wrapped up the paperwork on my desk, I received a call from Tonya, my previous secretary. I took a deep breath before I answered. I wasn't sure who to make it out to be. A thousand tiny thoughts pestered my brain in the brief ringing of the phone.

"Hello," I answered, expecting to hear Hitman's voice.

"Kingston, hey, it's me, Tonya."

"I know who it is Tonya. What do you need and why are you whispering?"

"I can't talk loud right now. He is in the other room sleeping, but I needed to talk to you for a minute."

"What is it? I'm kind of busy."

"I think that he knows about us. I can't be too sure, but the way he's been acting and the things that he's been saying have been off the wall. I'm scared for my life right now. I need to get away from here."

My attitude went from frustration to concern in the blink of an eye. Tonya's distressed call alarmed me. "Can you get away? If so, I can meet you and put you up for a while."

"No, I can't right now. It's too dangerous. I just need some money so that I can get out of town and never return."

"Whatever you need Tonya, just let me know."

"I just need to start anew somewhere. I don't want to know anyone or anything. I just want to get away. I need your help Kingston."

"Tonya, I will help you. Just come see me."

"I can't come to you, Kingston. I need you to meet me in a couple days. I will text you an address; just please meet me there with enough money to take care of our child and get me on my feet when I get there. Oh shit... he's waking up."

"Tonya…" I uttered out and, before I knew it, the call ended. "Fuck!" I yelled out.

How did I get myself into this shit? My dick was starting to put me in more situations than I could keep up with. I sat at my desk massaging my temples, when my phone rang again.

"Tonya…" I answered hurriedly.

"No, Mr. Kennedy, this is Raul from CPR."

"Who?" I questioned.

"Raul, from cellphone repair. You dropped an IPhone off with us. I was calling to tell you that we have gotten it unlocked and it'll be ready for pickup whenever you get here."

I pondered for a second until I realized who exactly it was that I was talking to.

"Thank you. I will be headed your way this evening."

"Mr. Kennedy, we will see you when you arrive. Your total charge is $148. We will see you soon."

The call disconnected and I returned to my position, trying to get my brain to shut off. I needed Tahleea in the worst way. Not so much for the sexual release, but she was someone I could talk to about anything. I couldn't believe I was such an idiot and destroyed what we had.

I gathered my things to prepare myself to leave. Upon me entering the elevator, my phone rang once more. It was a number I hadn't seen before. I tried to answer, but the elevator jammed the signal. Once downstairs, I tried to call it back, but I got no answer. I thought nothing more of it. It wasn't the first time they'd called, but they never left a voicemail the other times. It couldn't have been as important as it had seemed. Before leaving the parking lot, I sent a text to India.

Italian for dinner? -Kingston

The past few days at home have been rough, but we were trying to remain cordial with one another. The fact that she was pregnant was the underlining there because had she not been, KJ and I would've been gone. I still hadn't received an honest answer from her as to why she felt the need to lie to me about anything, but I was at a point that I didn't care anymore. I wanted to take as much stress off her as possible until the baby came. It was going to be a long ass ride, but hearing my child crying coming from her womb was going to be worth it.

IDC. Whatever you want. -India

I took her comment as a yes and proceeded to handle the business that I needed to. I pulled out of the parking lot and into traffic. As I made my way into the shopping plaza where the cellphone repair shop was, my phone began to buzz again. It was the strange number.

"Hello."

No one spoke a word.

"Hello," I uttered again.

Still nothing.

"Tahleea."

Just as those words parted my lips, the call ended. My breath was taken away. A part of me was unsure if it was her; yet, my heart began to race, indicating that it was. She was at least still alive and, if it was her, I was on her mind. Exhaling, I got out of my car and made my way into the store.

"Welcome to CPR."

"Yes, I received a phone call that a phone I dropped off was ready."

The young Korean man looked at me, then at the computer screen. "What's the name?"

"Kennedy… Kingston Kennedy."

"Oh, yeah man, give me one second. I have to go in the back and grab it."

I pulled my cell out and began to read over emails that I received. I had a client sending over last minute attachments and needed to review them. Moments later, he resurfaced. He looked at the phone, making sure that the screen was no longer locked.

"Yo, Mr. K., here you go man." He handed me the phone with a gigantic smile on his face, almost giggling like a school age child.

"What's so funny?" I asked.

"Nothing's funny man." He began to rub his hands together as he spoke his peace. "I just want to be like you when I grow up man. You got the look of a business man, but some of the content of that phone show me you a true player man."

I smirked at him and tipped my head. He handed me one of his business cards, as I turned to walk out. I didn't know what he saw on the phone, but it was enough to have him intrigued and I myself was curious to know.

I got to my car and began to scroll through Mario's emails and messages. It was all pretty much the same shit I had seen, with the exception of some generic emails. That's when shit got real. I opened an email from Tahleea. It was older, but it was a plea to her husband, asking him to fix their broken relationship and marriage. It was almost as if she was trying to salvage something that was dead. Some of the content touched home and the rest I let go. I knew how she felt about me and nowhere in the email did I get the feeling that she was still in love with him. She just wanted peace in their home. Upon me closing the email out, I noticed that there was one in the sent box labeled 'for your eyes only'. It was sent to my wife's work email.

I opened the attachment and it was a video of Mario stroking his dick for her. I immediately closed out the attachment and placed the phone on the seat next to me.

"Ok… breathe, Kingston. Maybe it was a mistake and he didn't mean to send that to her."

I had to calm myself down because mistakes happened, I knew that. I picked the phone back up and went to the search bar of the email page. I typed in her work email and, to my surprise, there was over a thousand message between the two of them. I swallowed my spit as I skimmed over some of the subject matters. My heart was breaking by the moment. Some of the emails dated as far back as four years ago.

I opened the picture gallery and noticed that this nigga had an entire gallery dedicated to my wife titled Ikea. There were so many fucking pictures of my wife spread eagle and sucking this nigga's dick that I couldn't help but to cry. I couldn't believe my eyes. I had been betrayed in my own fucking home. This bitch had this nigga on my couch and in my bed. I felt death cover my body as I exhaled flames.

I placed the phone seat and punched my dashboard. I had to compose myself before I made an irrational decision when I got home. I decided to go ahead and get dinner so that I could give myself a few minutes to calm down. I began to get a migraine, thinking about the phone. I grabbed it and powered it back down, placing it in my pocket.

When I got home, I placed dinner on the counter. I placed both hands on the granite counter top and took a deep breath. The feel of my home was not the same. I allowed another tear to fall before composing myself. I loosened my tie, then yelled for my son.

"KJ, COME EAT!" My voice boomed throughout the house and it was enough to bring India out of our bedroom.

"Kingston, is everything ok? Why are you yelling at him like that?"

I turned to look at her but couldn't say a word. She looked into my eyes and could see that they had been crying. They were as red as the flames in hell

"Kingston, what's wrong?"

"I'm fine."

She walked over and tried to place her hands on my back. "No, you're not," she stated as she took her fingertips caressing my spine.

"Don't touch me!" I barked, turning around and moving her hands.

"Kingston."

KJ came running into the kitchen like a bat out of hell. "Daddddddy!"

I picked him up and held him tight, as I stared down India. "Fix his plate and mine. I'm going to change."

She looked at me but did as I commanded. I placed KJ firmly back onto his own two feet and had him sit down. Walking into my bedroom, I could feel the emotions overwhelming me once again.

How could she do this to me? I wasn't innocent by any stretch of the imagination, but I was warranted in my reasoning for cheating or so I thought. I began to remove my clothes as I heard the bedroom door open.

"Baby, your food is ready. Are you sure you're ok?"

"Yes, I'm fine, stop asking me that fucking question."

She closed the door and stepped in. She had been lounging around for most of the day it seemed, as she covered herself with her robe.

“Ok, Kingston. I need you to talk to me. I know shit has been rocky lately, but I am here for you. I haven’t seen you like this in years.”

“Bit…” I took a deep breath and stopped myself. I didn’t want to make a scene while KJ was home. “India, right now isn’t the time. I just want to eat, drink a beer, and watch tv.”

She turned her nose up and decided that it was best to leave me alone.

I followed her into the kitchen with so many thoughts of bashing her fucking brains in, but that wasn’t the impression I needed my son to have of me. She sat at one end of our table and I sat at the other.

The room was filled with silence. The constant clicking of forks hitting plates were the only sounds made. KJ broke the silence, as his high-pitched voice filled the room.

“So, daddy, how was your day? What did you do?”

I looked at my son and smiled, trying to hold back the tears. “My day was good buddy. How was your day?”

“My day was splendiferous.”

My eye ducts watered more as he spoke. “Splendiferous, huh? That’s a big word. Where you learn it?”

“Mommy and me were watching Sesame Street and it was the word of the day,” he spoke, flinging food all over the table.

“Don’t chew with your mouth open,” she spoke in his direction, as she reached for her phone in the pocket of her robe.

"No phones at the table," I stated while placing my fork to my mouth, burning a hole through her heart.

"How was your day mommy?" KJ asked, breaking yet another awkward exchange.

"My day was great baby. I got to spend it with my favorite guy, then my second favorite guy made it home and brought dinner so that I wouldn't have to make anything. I just love my men."

I inhaled, then exhaled an enormous amount of air. Her bullshit was filling the room faster than the air could circulate. "Excuse me."

Getting up from the table, I walked into the bathroom. I could no longer contain my emotions as the tears flowed into the sink. India walked in to check on me after a few moments had passed.

"Ok, Kingston, seriously, what is it baby?" she asked once more, placing her hand on my back. "You haven't cried in years. What can I do?"

I looked in the mirror at her and gritted my teeth. "You can give me a DNA test and divorce me."

"Excuse me?" she questioned.

I turned around so that I could get a good look into her face. "I want a divorce and I want a paternity test done on KJ."

"Ok Kingston, I know I've lied in the past couple weeks about some shit, but don't you think testing our 3-year-old is a bit much? I'm not going to put him through that."

"Why? What are you afraid of? Are you scared that he belongs to the same nigga that this one does?"

She looked appalled at my statement and slapped my face. "How fucking dare you, Kingston Kennedy? I am your wife and the mother of your children."

I looked at her and hell froze still. I felt my hand ball up and, before I could swing, KJ walked in.

"Mommy… Daddy… please don't fight."

India turned and picked him up off the ground. I turned, walked over to the clothing I removed, and took Mario's phone out. I placed it on the bed.

"All your answers are in the emails and photo gallery. I'm done."

I kissed KJ and stormed out of the room. I got into my car and pushed the pedal down to the floor board. I was dead on the inside. The one thing that I loved more than myself was possibly someone else's.

As I came to a red light, I grabbed my cellphone and texted the mysterious number that had been calling me.

Tahleea, I don't know if this is you but, in the event it is, I NEED YOU. I am sorry for hurting you and destroying your trust in me. Baby, I love you and the last thing that I wanted was for my truth to hurt you. I just needed to be up front with you. If this is you, please come home. I NEED YOU! -Kingston

Chapter 20

India

I sat on the edge of our bed, sulking in my thoughts and tears as I scrolled through the emails and text messages of the phone Kingston left behind. I stared at myself pitifully in all the explicit pictures that I had sent Memphis on several occasions. How could I be so dumb and selfish by doing such disloyal things to my husband? All Kingston had ever done was love me unconditionally and took care of our family. He worshipped the ground that I walked on and, yet, I repaid him by being a filthy whore and cheating with a man whom didn't even appreciate himself, let alone me. The pain in Kingston's eyes hurt me to the core, and I despised myself for inflicting such lacerations on his heart. Now, he wanted a DNA test on our son, but who was I to blame him? With all the lies that I had told and secrets I had hidden, I was lucky that he hadn't killed my ass.

I had put KJ to bed early because I was an emotional wreck and I didn't want him to see me in that state. I didn't know how I would live without my husband, but I had to figure out because I knew for sure that we were over; there wasn't any coming back from this situation. My emotions flopped back and forth from angry to sad, as I tried to understand how my marriage got to this point. What's done in the dark always came to light, so I knew that my actions would catch up with me sooner or later. I just didn't expect it to happen the way that it did. I couldn't even understand how Kingston got a hold of Memphis' phone but, at this point, it didn't even matter. The damage was already done and I had to face my consequences. Getting up from the bed and walking over to the dresser, I grabbed my phone and commenced to call up Memphis. I really didn't want to be with him, but he would soon have to become KJ and I's financial stability, so I had to reel him in and butter him up.

Dialing his number, I placed the phone to my ear and waited for him to answer. After several rings, it went to his voicemail. I hung up and called right back and, that time, it rung twice and he sent me to voicemail.

"Fuck!" I screamed aloud, running both hands through my hair as I paced my bedroom floor. I was stressed the fuck out and I really needed someone to talk to. Running downstairs to our bar, I grabbed a bottle of red wine and a glass and headed to our entertainment room. I was pissed that I was pregnant because with the shit that I had on my brain, I needed something way stronger. Plopping down onto the sofa, I opened the bottle and filled my glass. I quickly gulped it down and poured another. Picking my phone back up, I tried calling Memphis again and he sent me to voicemail again. I huffed heavily out of frustration, as I couldn't understand why the bastard was steady ignoring my calls. I decided to give it a rest and try again in the morning. If he would continue to ignore me, I was going to be at his house as soon as I dropped KJ off to school.

Chapter 21

Tahleea

The hospital let me go the same night and I was more than grateful. They filled me up with fluids and gave me a prescription for some prenatal vitamins and iron pills. I had been calling Kingston over and over but hadn't got an answer. It was starting to piss me off because I really needed to speak with him. It was okay though because while I was in the hospital, I had looked up flights and was able to get one back to Seattle first thing in the morning. I was going to go straight to his office as soon I settled in.

Getting up from the king-sized bed in my hotel room, I pulled out my luggage and began to pack my things. I couldn't wait to get back home. I knew I would have to deal with Memphis and his bullshit but, honestly, I was just prepared to tell him I wanted a divorce. I had nothing to lose. He had already signed his life over to Kingston, so I had the upper hand. I owned my boutique and part of his studio; his ass was done for. Chuckling on the inside, I imagined the look on his face when he found out how much of a dummy his ass was. He thought he was signing a million-dollar deal, all the while getting fucked with no Vaseline.

After packing all my stuff, I made my way to the bathroom so that I could shower. I had to be at the airport at 4 a.m., so I wanted to make sure that I was prepared. Stripping out of my clothes, I reached over and turned the shower on. While I waited for the water to get warm, I stared at myself in the mirror. I ran my hand over my belly and began to smile. I wasn't far along enough for a pudge, but just knowing that I was carrying a part of Kingston inside of me made my world go around. I was going to do everything in my power to make sure I had a healthy pregnancy so that I could carry the baby full-term.

Stepping into the shower, I let the soothing hot water shoot all over my body. I inhaled deeply then exhaled, as it felt like the stress left my body with every bead of water that hit my skin. Grabbing my Neutrogena Rainbath Ocean Mist body wash, I lathered up my exfoliating sponge and began washing my body. After cleaning myself thoroughly two times, I rinsed off good and got out. Drying my body, I wrapped the towel around me and headed back into the room. After moisturizing up with Jergens Daily Moisture body lotion, I put on some panties and a tank top and climbed into the bed. Reaching over onto the nightstand, I tuned off the lamp and, before I knew it, I was knocked out.

****

My flight touched down in Seattle around 7:45 a.m. After retrieving my things from baggage claim, I made my way to the airport garage to get my car. I then packed all my suitcases in and hopped into the driver's seat. Starting up my engine, I sat there for a minute and let my car warm up, since it had been sitting for a week and a day. While I waited, I pulled out my cell and powered it on. It immediately began to go off, repeatedly alerting me of missed calls, emails, and text messages. I noticed that Kingston attempted to call me back; then, I noticed a text message from him. Quickly pulling it up, I began reading it.

Tahleea, I don't know if this is you but, in the event, it is I NEED YOU. I am sorry for hurting you and destroying your trust in me. Baby, I love you and the last thing that I wanted was for my truth to hurt you. I just needed to be up front with you. If this is you, please come home. I NEED YOU! -Kingston

Tears instantly began to fill my eyes as I felt the sincerity in his message. I missed my baby so much and I couldn't wait to be in his presence. I could smell the warm scent of his cologne and his breath on my skin. I hated that I let my emotions get the best of me and made us stay apart for so long. I had to get back to my man immediately. Clicking on his name, I hurriedly called him up. My ears began to heat up as his phone went straight to voicemail. Taking deep breath, I hung up and called right back to only get the same thing.

"Ugggh!" I screamed out, then punched my steering wheel. This phone tag shit was beginning to drive me insane. Going back to his text message, I read it once more, then sent my own.

Kingston, baby, I'm here. I miss you so much and I just wish you would pick up the phone so that I can talk to you. I'm so sorry for walking out on you without hearing you out. I love you so much baby and I can't see my life without you. I'm going home to get settled. Call me as soon as you get this message so that we can meet up at our spot. -Tahleea

I pressed send, sat my phone into the cup holder, and drove out of the airport garage headed to my home. I was driving like a bat out of hell, so I made it there in no time. Pulling into the garage, I noticed Memphis' truck and immediately prepared for war. I knew once I stepped foot into the door, he was going to start acting a fool, wondering where I had been for the last week. Reaching onto the back seat, I grabbed my purse, then exhaled heavily as I got out and approached the door. Putting my key into the door, I tried to turn it but noticed that it didn't work.

"No, this stupid muthafucka didn't change the locks on my ass!" I said aloud to myself, as I began banging on the door like a mad woman. I then turned around and began kicking it like the white boy Roach from off Next Friday. I was thirty-eight hot, and Memphis had me fucked up if he thought he could just change locks on my ass. After a couple of minutes of my loud banging, the door flew open and

Memphis stood behind it in his Ralph Lauren robe, with the look of death upon his face. Any other time I would've been petrified but, for some reason, his punk ass didn't scare me one bit. I sized him up and down with a mean scowl plastered upon my face, letting him know that he didn't put fear in me anymore and that I was fed up with his shit.

"Move Memphis, let me in!" I spat, sucking my teeth. He slightly chuckled, then quickly put his mean mug back on.

"Bitch, please! You no longer live or welcomed back into my house again. You disappear for a week, change your number, didn't call, text, or shit, and you come back to my shit like it's all good!? Hoe, you must've lost yo muthafuckn mind!" he seethed through gritted teeth.

"Okay, cool. Just let me get the rest of my things and I'm out. You can have this fuckin house and everything else; I just want a divorce," I said nonchalantly. Memphis thought he was hurting me by telling me that I couldn't come back to that house, but he was really making my burdens lighter. After I got my shit, he wouldn't have to worry about seeing or hearing from my ass again, unless it was about signing them papers.

"Bitch, you ain't getting shit else up out of here, so you can just take yo hoe ass back to where ever the fuck you been for the past week. Whatever shit you tryna get, you should've got that shit when you ran off the first fuckin time! Fuck you, Tahleea, get the fuck from away from my door bitch!" he stated and tried to close the damn door in my face. Before I knew it, I had reacted and put my foot into the door, and he quickly opened it back up, looking at me as if I were insane.

"Bitch, you must want to a..."

"I JUST WANT MY FUCKIN SHIT MEMPHIS! NOW, LET ME THE FUCK IN SO I CAN GET IT!" I tuned the fuck up on his ass in the blink of an eye, kicking the door wide open and bussing him in the mouth. Blood instantly began to leak from the hole in his face as he spit up his two front teeth. Barging into our home, I quickly ran up the steps to the closet. I went straight for my safe and grabbed my stun gun that I had bought a while ago but never used it. I knew Memphis would be up the steps in no time to get his revenge, and I was ready to fry his ass the fuck up. Just as I suspected, he came busting into the bedroom, screaming in rage with blood flying from his mouth.

"Bitch, I'ma kill yo slut bucket ass!" he said, charging toward me. As soon as he was in arm's reach, I pulled the taser from behind my back, stuck it to his rib cage, and his ass began to shake like a stripper on a Friday night. He immediately hit the floor as he began to scream out, cursing me even more.

"Aaaahhh, you stupid BITCH! I'M GONNA FUCKIN KILL YOU! YOU A DEAD BITCH, YOU DEAD AS FUCK!" he screamed at me, and I gave him one hard kick to his growing area, causing him to hurdle over and began vomiting.

"FUCK YOU, MEMPHIS. I'M SICK OF YOUR SHIT! I HATE YOU AND I WISH I NEVER MET YO SICK ASS!" I screamed as I began to kick him over and over. I then stuck the taser to his ass again and cooked his ass up a lil more. Memphis began to piss and shit on himself, as I held the stun gun to his ass until I felt like letting up. When I did decide to release him, he just laid there still in his own blood, piss, feces, and vomit. I kicked him once more and he didn't budge. Reaching down, I touched his neck; he still had a pulse. The nigga wasn't dead; he was just fucked up. I was a bit relieved because my future was too bright to be catching a murder charge.

Running back into the closet, I began to quickly grab all my things, dumping them into luggage and bags.

"Memphis! Memphis, baby, are you here? Why is the door wide open?" I heard a familiar voice calling in the distance, and my body immediately froze up.

"Mario! Where are you, baby? Stop playing, we need to talk." The voice began to get closer, as I heard heels clicking up our steps and towards our bedroom. I remained silent and as still as possible, trying not to make a sound.

"It's me, India, baby. Come out and stop messing around. I'm not in the mood to be playing. I need to talk to you about Kingston and I; he knows about us." The voice continued, and my blood instantly began to boil all over again. I had to be going crazy with my mind, playing trick on me.

"Memph… noooo, oh my God; Mario, baby, get up! What happened to you?" She quickly ran to his aid and kneeled beside him. Picking up his upper body, she cradled him in her arms as she checked to make sure that he was still breathing.

"Oh, my God, Mario; baby, please wake up! Who did this to you? Wake up please, we have a baby to raise!" she cried, as I watched her from behind the crack of the door of the closet. My heart began to race as uncontrollable anger fueled my body. This bitch had been sleeping with my husband, all while skinning and grinning in my face like nothing was happening. I began to chuckle on the inside because it was funny how that hoe Karma worked. I was screwing her husband and pregnant by him, and she was screwing and pregnant by mine. Her ass didn't know about us though, but I knew about them now and she wasn't going to get away with it.

I watched as India grabbed her purse and began fumbling through it for something. She then pulled out her phone, and I automatically assumed that she was calling 911.

"Put that fucking phone down; he don't need no help, his punk ass is breathing!" I seethed, stepping out of the closet and startling the hell out of her. She looked up at me like a deer caught in headlights, as she took a hard swallow.

"Tah, Tahleea... hey... hey girl, what you doing here? I... I thought you were away," she stated, stuttering over her words. I immediately scoffed.

"Don't fuckin hey girl me, you trifling ass bitch! What am I doing here? Nah, the question is what the fuck is your tramp ass doing here?" I spat, getting closer into her space. She began to slowly get up and back away from me.

"I... I... can explain," she said, holding her hands up in surrender. I could tell that the bitch was scared out of her mind.

"Explain what? WHAT HOE?! Explain how yo filthy slut ass was fucking my husband and, now, you're pregnant by his sorry ass?!" I barked. "Shit, to be honest, I don't give two flying fucks. You can have his woman abusing ass; you just took away my problems. The only thing that I'm upset about is that you knew you were screwing him and you still tried to befriend me," I continued, glaring at her with evil eyes.

"No, no, I promise T, it wasn't like that," she stated. I instantly let out a crazy chuckle.

"Oh, I'm sorry. I got it wrong? Then, what was it like then?" I asked calmly, still walking towards her. I wasn't going to tase her because I knew that she was pregnant and I wanted her to have that baby so that she could deal with Memphis and all the misery that came with him; but, I was going to smack her the fuck up for thinking that she could just play me like I was some type of video game.

"Just please, hear me out, pl…" I backhanded the shit out of her in midsentence, and she instantly grabbed her face in astonishment. I then snatched her up, wrapping her long flowing weave around my hand and began banging her face into the wall a good three times, causing her to instantly blackout and hit the floor.

Leaving her laid next to her punk ass baby daddy, I grabbed my shit and got the fuck out of that house. After throwing all my shit into my car, I got in and immediately called the hotel that me and Kingston spent our time at. I requested the room that we'd always got and the lady told me that it was already occupied. Right then, I knew that my baby must've been already staying there because that room was never taken. Ending the call with the hotel clerk, I hurriedly sent Kingston a text.

I know where you are. Stay there, I'm on my way baby! -Tahleea

I sent the message and did the dash to go see my man.

Chapter 22

Memphis

Nursing my wounds in the aftermath of hurricane Tahleea, India sat next to me on the end of the bed. Awkwardly, the two of us just stayed in silence for a moment, until she reached into her purse. She handed me my old phone and began to cry.

"He knows everything," she stated.

I looked dumbfounded. How did she have my phone and what did she mean by that?

"What the fuck are you talking about India?"

"He knows about our affair, he's seen the pictures, the messages… he's seen it all."

I swiped the screen and, to my surprise, it opened right up. How the nigga ended up with my phone, I didn't know? Somehow, the motherfuckers managed to get past the lock screen I had on the phone. I placed the phone on the bed and took the frozen pack of steak and placed it back on my side.

"When I do catch Tahleea's ass, she's going to wish that she would have stayed away," I spoke.

India was as pale as a ghost sitting next to me. I leaned over and placed my hand on her back. "This is what we wanted, right?" I asked, taking my other hand and rubbing her stomach.

"Not like this. I didn't see it coming like this. I feel so stupid."

I shook my head and turned away from her. I couldn't believe that now she was trying to back away from our situation. This shit wasn't new and it was only a matter of time before it got to this point anyway.

"I hate to ask right now, but I'm going to need that money faster than I thought."

I looked at her with a side eye. She had me fucked up if she thought she was going to see a penny of it back. "I ain't got it."

She dropped her head, took a deep breath, and let a few tears fall from her eyes.

"I don't know what I'm going to do. I have some money, but Kingston was my stability. He took care of my needs, while I took care of my wants. I can't afford to live alone."

"Just get your shit and move in here. I'm pretty sure that, after this, Tahleea ain't coming back to me. Just let Kingston get custody of that lil bastard of his and we can build our own empire here with our lil one."

I rubbed her stomach, thinking that my idea was foolproof. India got quiet for a moment, as she thought about my request.

"As nice as that sounds, I decline. I can't afford to have her double back and do this shit all over again and, hell no, I'm not giving up custody of my son. Hell, he might not be Kingston's."

"India, what the hell you mean, he might not be Kingston's? Who the fuck is the father?"

She looked deep into my eyes and I already knew. Shocked by her silence, I sat and placed one of my hands over my head.

"Let's just let shit rest where it may. I don't want to think any more on this. We've fucked up enough. It's best if we stay in separate places for a while."

I didn't expect the words she spoke. I didn't think that she did either, but I understood where she came from. It was all news to me. I'd been wanting an heir to my throne and, the entire time, I had one being raised by another nigga.

"So, what now?" I asked her.

She was just as clueless as I was, as we sat in the silent room. Her phone began to ring. From the sounds of it, it was enough to make her leave in a hurry.

"I'll be back eventually. Keep your phone on you. I have to go. That was my nanny, something has happened to KJ. He's gone."

"I'm coming with you."

She shook her head no and darted for the door. In the blink of an eye, she was gone and I was left alone, stuck with my thoughts momentarily. It took a second to register, but I got up from my place and followed her. Something major had to happen because she sprinted out of the house. Shit had finally hit the fan and all hell was breaking loose.

Chapter 23

Kingston

An emotionally unstable wreck, I sat on the bed with a bottle of Hennessy, attempting to leave all my feelings in the bottom of it. The images burned into my head of my wife fucking another man wouldn't go away. My phone was powered off. I wanted to be alone. Tahleea was missing, KJ possibly wasn't mine, and my secretary birthed my son. I had everything a man could want in life, but my secrets were beginning to kill me from the inside out. The effect of the liquor began to work as the walls started to close in on me. I began breathing heavily. The once full bottle was down to less than a quarter.

I heard a knock on the door and stood to my feet. "Who is it?" I yelled, slurring the phrase.

"Baby, open up. It's me."

I couldn't make out the voice as I stumbled over to the door.

"Kingston, open up baby, it's me. Tahleea."

I began to weep. The liquor was making me hallucinate. I couldn't understand what was going on. If this was my karma, then this bitch was winning. I heard the knocking at the door again.

"Leave me alone!" I yelled out.

"Kingston, baby, please open the door."

I placed my head against the wooden door, not knowing what to expect on the other side. I took a deep breath and touched the handle. I prayed that I wasn't losing my mind and that it was in fact someone on the other side of the door. Wiping the tears from her eyes, I exhaled while staring Tahleea in the face. She reached out and wrapped her arms around me, crying. I was in shock as I pushed her backwards.

"Don't ever fucking leave me like that again. I've missed you."

I pulled her back into me and held her tightly. The door closed and the two of us spent what seemed like an eternity embraced in one another's grasp. I scooped her up and took her over to the bed. She kept her arms wrapped around my neck and kissed my lips as gently as she possibly could. Without hesitation, I returned the favor. I'd missed the taste of her.

Things began to escalate. The Hennessey intensified my senses. I was no longer all over the place. All my energy was placed in one area and that was pleasing Tahleea. I removed my shirt and the heat of the moment intensified exponentially. I undressed her body gently, removing her clothing. I placed her body on my lap facing me, as I centered myself in the middle of the bed.

My breaths clung to her skin as I placed several kisses upon her body. Her body lusted for mine, as I began to gently bite her skin. I took a handful of her hair and pulled her head back so that she could release her desires into the air. She sighed out, as I placed one of her perky breast in my mouth. There was a distinct taste that she had, but I paid it no mind as the two of us prepared for war.

Lifting her up slightly, my dick parted her lips and began penetrating her insides. "Don't ever leave me again," I whispered in an airy sigh.

She didn't reply with words; she simply allowed my dick to fill her as she worked up and down, finding a rhythm that worked for her. As we got deeper in to the session, I found myself wrapped up in her. Not so much the physical part, but the mental aspect. We were in sync on so many levels and it only elevated our love making.

As the song changed to Tank's *Close*, so did the position we were in. I laid her body flat on the bed, keeping her legs wrapped around my waist. I placed one of the pillows beneath her ass and took my hands, placing it gently on top of her pelvis as I stroked in and out of her. I placed my thumb against her clit and gently moved it in circles.

"Shit, Kingston," she sighed out as she began to feel the sensation taking control of her body. I could feel my dick working her, as I applied a little more pressure on her pelvis.

"Kingston I… shit…"

In a matter of moments, her pussy was gushing over my dick. She'd cum for me like she never had before. As she did, I felt myself slipping. I leaned over and began to give her long deep strokes. I placed my forehead against hers and looked into her eyes. With every long, deep, purpose-filled stroke, I solidified that she was where I wanted her to be. The deeper I dug into her, the more we connected.

She took her nails and scratched my face, beginning to feel the pressure building behind my thrust. She sucked my bottom lip and the tears began to roll from the both of our eyes. I began to pick my pace up. I was flowing with the song and getting closer to the mountain top. She was right there with me.

"I'll never leave you again baby. I… I… love you…"

Just as she uttered those words, my dick released and everything I had left was implanted in her. Lying in her while allowing my dick to throb, I kissed her.

"I love you," I replied.

I didn't want to move, but I knew that I had to. The past few days had already been way too emotional, but this topped the cake. The liquor was still fresh in my system and all I wanted to do now that I'd finally relaxed was sleep, and so did she. I rolled over and she placed her glistening face against my chest and dozed off.

When the two of us awoke from our nap, we gazed into one another's eyes. This was what was meant to be. The universe had spoken and she was here for me, as I for her. It was only right. I ran my hand across her beautiful face, removing the hair from it.

"I missed you," I mentioned as I moved closer to kiss her lips.

"I've missed you." She moved closer to me and got comfortable beneath me. "I'm sorry that I took off like I did, not really giving you a chance to explain everything."

I placed my finger over her lips, dispelling her comments. I didn't want to have any negative thoughts floating around. The moment was perfect in itself. I didn't want to have it ruined.

"No need to explain. What's done is done. As long as you are back here in my arms, then all is right. I love you."

She removed my hand from her lips and started to speak again. Just as she was about to begin, her phone began to ring. It was Mario. She gave off a slight smirk and chuckled.

"I can't believe his ass is really calling me," she answered and sat up in the bed. "Hello… nigga, fuck you and that bitch… I hope the both of you bitches die…" She hung up the phone and looked at me.

“I’m sorry about that Kingston. That’s a situation in itself that we need to discuss.”

With the way we just made love, I was honestly afraid to hear the words to come. I was for sure that she was coming to end things with me and return home to be a good wife to her dog ass nigga. I held my breath and looked into her eyes as she spoke.

“I hate to tell you this and it’s crazy as hell because of our situation, but your wife and my husband are fucking around with one another.”

Relieved, I shook my head and smiled in her direction. I tried to cover the pain but, honestly, it was a blow that was unexpected. I couldn’t say too much however, considering the arrangement her and I had.

“Yeah, I know. I found out recently. It’s been for a while.”

She could hear the pain in my voice as she placed her hand on my back. I kissed her forearm and rubbed her thigh.

“It is what it is. Karma has a way of showing you what its capable of. I can’t be mad, neither can you. We just have to charge it to the game.”

She took a deep breath and agreed. There were several things that we could have discussed, but there was no point to beat a dead horse. The past was in the rearview. I got up from the bed to go into the bathroom to take a piss, as she began to play on her phone.

Watching her, I walked over to my pants and pulled mine out, powering it on. As I relieved myself from the drunken, post-sex piss, I noticed that my voicemail box was overloading. Message after message was popping up from the visual voicemail application. I began to listen to the messages and most of them were from India crying, attempting to apologize for hurting me. I simply compiled every single one of them that had her number attached and batched them into the deleted folder. There was one from Tonya that alarmed me.

"Kingston. I need that money asap. I have to get away from him as fast as I possibly can. Please meet me at the address I am about to text to you."

Her message went silent for a moment, then I heard her phone drop.

"Who the fuck you in here whispering too, Tonya?" I could hear Hitman asking in the background right before the message ended.

I looked at the time of the message on the screen and noticed that it was less than 30 minutes ago when she called. There was a text notification with the address attached that I needed to meet her. There was also a text from India.

Kingston, I know that you're mad but something has happened to KJ. HE IS MISSING. I NEED YOU TO CALL ME ASAP. THIS IS NOT A GAME OR JOKE. 911. -India

I walked out of the bathroom and hurriedly dialed her number, but I got the voicemail twice. She had to be on some bullshit not to answer, so I thought nothing more of it. I grabbed my clothes off the floor and kissed Tahleea's forehead.

"Baby, I have to make a quick run."

She looked up at me from the bed, sitting up. "Is everything ok?"

"I don't exactly know, but I have to go find out."

“Well, I’m going to go with you. I’ve been away from you long enough. I can’t imagine another moment without you.”

“Well, let’s go. We can catch up on some things and talk on the way.”

The two of us left our room and headed towards the address given.

*****

Pulling up, I noticed that Tonya’s demeanor was nervous. I stepped out of my car while leaving it running and walked over to her.

“Tonya, what’s going on? Are you ok?”

“Kingston.” She burst in a tirade of tears as she lunged to hug me. “I am so sorry for everything.”

“What’s wrong? What’s going on?”

Just as I asked that question, I felt a presence and heard a set of feet walking up behind me.

“KINGSTON!” Tahleea yelled out from the passenger side of my car.

I felt a cold steel rod touch the back of my neck.

“My nigga. I’m glad you could join us. Now, you get explain to me why the fuck my wife has your son.”

From his words, Hitman had finally put two and two together. I looked into Tonya’s eyes before closing mine, saying a quick prayer. I couldn’t believe, after all the shit that I’d went through, that this was the way that I was about to go out. I could hear Tonya’s sobs and cries.

"Kingston, I am so sorry. Please forgive me. I never meant for this to happen."

"Shut the fuck up bitch," Hitman spat in her direction. "Go open the fucking trunk so that he can see who else gets to watch him die."

She shook her head no and he pointed the pistol in her direction.

"NOW! Don't make me ask again."

She walked to the back of her car and popped the trunk. Upon her closing it, I began to tear up. It was KJ. They had his hands bound and a bandana tied around his head, covering his mouth.

"Aye man, he ain't did shit; let him go."

"Nigga, shut the fuck up. I want him to see what pain feels like."

Hitman took his pistol and motioned for KJ to walk towards us. KJ ran over to me and jumped into my arms. I heard Hitman cock the hammer on his gun and I held my son tight, covering his face. Hitman leaned over and I could feel his breath in my ear as he placed the barrel on my temple.

"BANG!" he yelled, damn near making me lose my shit. He began to laugh as I stood before him shaken. "Damn man, I hope you didn't think that the party was done. I got more in store for you. See, I knew that if I took the seed, that the mother would follow. So, you get to tell her how you've been fucking my wife and well… she gets to tell you her secret."

He looked up and noticed a SUV coming around the corner. It stopped and, to Hitman's surprise, it was Mario.

"Well, I'll be damned. This shit is getting better by the minute. Everybody is in the same place. The gang's all here. Good. Glad you could join us Memphis. You too need to be here to witness the shit that's about to go down."

Hitman motioned towards Tonya and she opened the backdoor. India, too, was gagged and bound. Tonya removed the blindfold from India's eyes and pointed the gun at her, as she looked around with dried tear lines down her cheek. She noticed Mario on one side and I on the other.

"Oh, Mrs. Kennedy…" He walked over to her and placed the pistol into her cheek. "I don't think you know me, but I know you very well. You, Mrs. Kennedy, are the piece to the puzzle that connects us all. You have probably played the game the best."

"Hitman, bruh, what the fuck are you doing? Let her go man!" Memphis yelled.

Hitman pointed the pistol at him. "Bruh… brother… bro… nigga, yo ass lucky to still be breathing right now. I asked you for a little bit of help and you fucked me, my nigga. You had what I needed and YOU STILL FUCKED ME! I'm not mad though; I bet you didn't know that Kingston fucked you out of your studio."

Hitman looked in my direction and smirked, as he began to detail what he knew. I looked over at Memphis and dropped my head.

"Yeah nigga, he got yo ass. You don't own a single fucking piece to your own empire."

"What?" Memphis mumbled.

"Don't act surprised nigga. Shit, with the way you've been dicking his wife down and finessed her out of that money, you kind of deserve it. Ain't that right Mrs. Kennedy."

I looked over at India and it made sense. The money missing and the lying completely made sense now.

"But wait, there's more," Hitman stated like a crazed maniac. He began to giggle because he himself couldn't believe the fucked up degrees in which we were all connected here. "Kingston, don't look at her like that. Hell, it was his money to begin with. Bet you didn't know that I was the one that robbed you after the club that night, did you Memphis? Yeah, good ole Kingston decided that it would be an easy lick for me and that I would get a portion of the pot."

Memphis flinched and took a step towards me, and Hitman pointed his gun towards him.

"If he don't kill you, I am nigga," he seethed through his teeth.

I dropped my head and took a deep breath. "What is it that you want, Hitman? Name your price," I stated, trying to get him away from the subject.

"Oh no, it's too late for what I want. What I wanted was fifty thousand. What I wanted was my wife to not be pregnant by her fucking boss. What I wanted was to live happily ever after and provide for my family but, no, you had to come fuck that up and put that fertile ass dick in my bitch. So now, Kingston, I want blood. I want revenge. I want you to know the pain I've felt ever since your fucking son dawned this earth."

He pointed his gun towards KJ and fired in the dirt right next to him, making him scream.

"KJ!" India yelled, praying that he wasn't hit.

“Shut up with that damn screaming woman. I didn’t even graze the child. I’m not that fucking crazy. However, since everyone has secrets, I do have one of my own that I would like to share with my wife.”

He smiled in her direction and motioned for her to come to him. She did as he asked with tears in her eyes. He took her in his arms. He turned her body in a way that she was facing all of us. He then moved his forearm under her neck and began to squeeze.

“She’s beautiful, ain’t she?” he asked all of us as he placed his head against her temple. “I’ve loved you for a long time. There isn’t a day that goes by that I don’t. I’ve done everything for you, considering my situation. Day in and day out, I put my life on the line and you repay me by fucking someone else and having his child. If you were me, how would you feel? How would you react? I can’t have kids baby. That’s why you never got pregnant. I’m sterile. I can’t have kids. I got fixed after Kisha put me on child support.”

The fire and rage in Tonya’s eyes grew. She was pissed. He was killing her with verbal bullets as she stood in his grasp crying.

“I know you never meant to hurt me and all that bullshit, but the damage is done. I can’t begin to make you feel the way I do, but understand that I am about to try.” He began to squeeze her neck tighter, lifting her body off the ground. “I don’t want you to think that this shit is going to go unpunished. After I’m done with you, I’m going to your mother’s to kill that bastard child and, if she tries to stop me, she is going to feel my pain.”

I couldn’t sit still for long. Watching her body slowly lose its life didn’t sit well with me and, if it meant risking my life, then so be it. I stood to my feet and distracted Hitman long enough for him to release his grip on her.

“You serious right now nigga?” he asked in my direction. “Damn, I know she a good fuck, but are you willing to die for that pussy?”

I was done playing around with the situation. If it had to come down to someone dying, then I was sacrificing myself. I had nothing more to lose. Tahleea moved from her place and yelled for me.

“Kingston, I’m pregnant! The baby is yours!”

My heart stopped and I looked back towards her. Hitman rushed me. I was caught off guard, as the barrel of the pistol grazed my face. He and I tussled; my only goal was to wrestle the gun away from his hands. Once I got it away from him, I knew that I stood a chance. I grabbed his forearm and he began firing freely into the air.

Everyone ducked and India managed to grab KJ and get him out of harm’s way. I began to bite Hitman, which in turn made him drop the pistol. I saw it hit the dirt and I kicked it away from the both of us. He began to swing with the fury of ten me towards my face. I was able to get him off me, just enough to separate the two of us.

POW! POW! Two shots echoed out and Hitman grabbed his leg, attempting to see where the shots came from. Standing behind the smoking barrel was his wife, Tonya. She had tears flowing from her eyes as she stood over him.

“Bitch, are you serious right now?”

“Shut the fuck up.” She wiped her eyes and kept the pistol in plain sight for him to see. “I can’t believe you. All this time, I thought that there was something wrong with me. You’ve allowed me to go to doctors, specialists, and better. This whole time, you were the reason. Why didn’t you just tell me. I could have dealt with having no kids. WHY?" she screamed.

He didn't respond, which angered her more. "I've don't nothing but try to make sure that this marriage worked. Never once did I question you about what you did or how you provided. I allowed you to be the man of the house and, yet, you put my womanhood in question. You don't know what it feels like to love a man and not be able to give him a child. I cried too many nights for you to tell me this shit." She pulled the gun up and placed it right between his eyes. "As far as you killing me or my son, I won't give you the satisfaction."

She pulled the trigger and we all stood around in shock, looking at one another. Tonya had lost her cool and she felt betrayed by the acts and disloyalty of her husband. He knew that all she ever wanted was a family and he had stripped her from that right, all because of his no-good ass baby mother.

Tonya looked in the direction of all of us, as she went over and hugged KJ. "Baby boy, I am so sorry that you had to see that. I don't want you to ever feel like no one wants you. You are going to grow up and be someone special."

She kissed his forehead and dropped the pistol onto the ground. She walked towards me and wrapped her arms around my neck.

"Again, I am sorry for everything. Please forgive me."

"Tonya, I am sorry."

She wiped the tears from her eyes and backed away from me. Still in shock from the events transpired, we were frozen. She looked at the four of us and spoke her peace.

“What’s done in the dark comes to light. I hate that your son was a sacrifice,” she stated, looking in the direction of India. “But I need you all to take this as a lessoned learned. No secret is ever safe.”

THE END…

STAY TUNED FOR KINGSTON & TAHLEEA’S SPIN OFF!!! COMING SOON…2017

Check Out Other Great Books From Tiece Mickens Presents

Black And Blue 2: A Domestic Violence Love Story

Fatal Attraction

Rome And Harmony 2: An H-Town Love Story

Don't Play Russian Roulette With My Heart

She Puts The R In Ratchet 3

r

Made in the USA
Columbia, SC
23 July 2017